Flight of the Maita
Book 12a
Happy Birthday

The crew go adventuring. They discover the Freenz and experiment with the new TTH14 drive.

<u>Critic comment</u>
A lot like some earlier work.. I still do not like the M-82nds.
– PA Rtng: More than worth the price

Contents

About the author

CD was born in Lakeland, Florida, in 1938. He is educated in genetics and botany. He has traveled over much of the world, particularly when he was in music as a rock rhythm guitarist with some well-known bands in the late sixties and early seventies. He has worked as a high steel worker and as a longshoreman, clerk, orchidist, bar owner, salvage yard manager and landscaper – among other things.

CD began writing fiction in 1984 and has more than 300 books published as of 3/15/16 in SciFi, murder, orchid culture and various other fields.

He now resides in Puerto Armuelles, David, and Gualaca, Chiriqui, Panamá, where he continues research into epiphytic plants and plays music with friends. He loves the culture of the indigenous people and counts a majority of his closer friends among that group. Several have "adopted" him as their father. He funds those he can afford through the universities where they have all excelled. "The Indios are very intelligent people, they are simply too poor (in material things and money. Culturally, they are very wealthy) to pursue higher education."

CD loves Panamá and the people, despite horrendous experiences (Free e-book; *Fading Paradise*). He plans to spend the rest of his life in the paradise that is Panamá

- Estrelita Suarez V. de Jaramillo – 3/15/2016

CD is involved in research of natural cancer cure at this time. It has proven effective in all cases, so far. It is based on a plant that has been in use for thousands of years, is safe, available, and cheap. He has studied botany, and was cured of a serious lymphoma with use of the plant, *Ambrosia peruviana*.

Information about this cure is free on the FaceBook group, Natural medicine research. CD asks only that all who try it please report on its effectiveness on that group.

Happy Birthday!

<u>*Prologue*</u>

"Let me get this crap straight," Z (Steve Zutec, native of Terra) said. "You pull this hundred twenty fifth birthday party stunt just to break the news that Louahna has some little problem for us?

"Maita! You know we're all about to go nuts from sitting around here! Who needs the ruse?"

Louahna was a being from another galaxy who had partially been transferred into another dimensional plane on the trip to this galaxy. She and a few fellow refugees from the exploding galaxy called M82 by the astronomers of Terra when Z was first abducted were now contacting developing cultures in this galaxy to attempt to instill certain positive qualities in them. They had long ago learned their own deaths would mean a devastating planal implosion and also that there was no way they could ever breed in two planes.

They decided on a unique way to fight the boredom of their unintentional immortality. It helped that they could "step" into their second plane at any point within the energy sphere of this galaxy and "step" back into N (Normal) space at any other point they chose.

On Earth one of them had been known as Merlin. His real name was Zianteus and he was now working, among his several other present projects, with Joe's People on EC (Empire Center), but that was a different story. That's several different stories, in fact.

Maita was many things: It was basically a spaceship and the computers that ran the ship, the emperor of the Maitan

Empire (That's a library full of stories), the leader of a crew of assorted beings and a close friend of all those people. It was amazingly learned and intelligent (It was well over two thousand Maitan Empire years old) compassionate and caring and had a great sense of humor. The Terran, Z, had forced both it and Thing to develop their senses of humor or forever be confused about what he was doing and why.

Thing was a Mentan (Z's name for their planet) empath who was kidnapped by a race of insectoids along with Z and four others, but that's also another story. It was a small, squarish, rubbery ball with four tentacles and eyes on short stalks. The eyes worked independently, which could be disconcerting to beings whose eyes focused together.

Thing communicated with an empathic talent.

Both Maita and Thing used the speakers all over the ship and those on gravitic floaters Thing was often riding (It also rode around on Z or Tab's shoulders quite often. Tentacles are *not* designed to move well on the smooth surfaces that comprise most of a spaceship) to speak with Z or other organic beings. The system they used was a bell tone (* – *) before and after Maita's words and a tuning fork sound ([–]) before and after Thing's words.

Another thing the crew was now used to was that one had to listen to the words of Thing and/or Maita carefully. They used no inflection or intonation, thus everything they said tended to be in the form of one long paragraph. There was no real distinction between separate thoughts. Z was so used to it now he no longer noticed it. He'd listened to them for more than ninety empire years and learned to expect the form.

Tab, the last of the regular "crew", was a mechanical being who was manufactured by Maita, ostensibly to do detective work for the empire. He was built in the form of a Swaz (An amphibian being from a planet called Swaville), and only the immediate crew and the M82nds (The sound of their racial name in phonetic Maitan was an extremely vulgar, even obscene term, thus "M82nd" was used) knew, now that Tranz (A Kheth diplomat) was dead.

The temporary members of "Maita's crew" knew from time to time, but few of them were now living.

Tab's ship, TRD-60 (TR for short) was actually part of Tab (and vice versa) at most times because they were linked through strange band gravitics and radio except at times when they must cease the communication where someone may have any sensors that could intercept the transmissions, thus discovering the secret.

Each had its distinct personality at the same time making them a sort of schizophrenia.

The Zulians and Parf knew Tab was a machine, but those are other stories, too.

Tab was built with a sense of humor, and was able to learn vastly more than most organics because the connections with TR could store fantastic amounts of data. The two "brains" could link to become a super brain few could hope to equal. TR could simply add a few cubic meters of memory chips and store and process another galaxy's knowledge. TR's increases built Tab's abilities at the same time.

Tab could be modified greatly in the shops in TR and Maita to pass for any number of different races of various kinds of beings in the empire. Z could also be modified in the medical facilities on the ships to pass for various mammalian races.

Thing couldn't be modified to any great extent because of its critical internal pressures. It was from a planet with extreme atmospheric pressure, which made it tough and able to withstand the pressures under kilometers of water or to live in a vacuum for a few minutes. Maita had augmented its skin, eyes, etc. greatly. It breathed through membranes that were as efficient in water as in air (Now. Maita had augmented them a little). It was physically inflexible as to form, but could live in the different conditions that made up for it.

The summons from Louahna isn't a trick. It's meant partly as a birthday present! I'm going a bit nutzo myself sitting around here.

"We all are!" Tab agreed. "I haven't had even a simple case to work on in half a year.

"Where do we have to go to meet Louahna?"

Z's jaws tightened a bit, but he said nothing. Thing looked at him, then away.

Neeahna. Maybe Zianteus can tell us why she doesn't make it Neeneeahna?

The fuzzy outline that was Zianteus had been hovering around the edge of the pool to the side of the entrance to Z's home. Z had, with the help of the famous Parf artist, Tous, built the place on his personal island on EC. It was like living inside of a fantastic painting.

"This is all news to me," Zianteus protested. "I suppose she's brought something for you to see so she wants to show it on her own planet."

[She probably found some new orchid-like plant to show Z. Does she know it's his birthday today?]

"How in the nine hells would she know that?" TR snapped through the speakers (None of the crew could figure how a machine using a synthetic voice over remote speakers could get such finely-tuned inflections into the vocalizations – particularly considering it had been designed and built by a machine that very seldom did so itself!).

[Stick it in your moder!]

They weren't angry at one another. This was one of the games they often played.

Z's father had been an orchid and bromeliad grower on Earth and Z had collected many plants that resembled them on many worlds. He also had thousands of varieties from Earth itself. He had even been able to mericlone and replant species that had become extinct on Earth.

When the group originally met Louahna they found she was also a grower and collector of the same types of plants on her own world, Neeahna. She lived on her own private continent there.

"I doubt that, Thing," Z said. "She would've brought it here. There's only one way to find out what she wants! We leave as the red sun rises?" (EC has three differently colored suns placed in a triangular configuration with EC at the center of gravity. The race who moved the stars and planoformed the world were dead, but that's also another story.)

"Yo!" TR replied quickly. "I take it I can tag along? I'm about to go black hole from inaction myself!"

[You always were out of it! Your whole excuse for a brain is a black hole!]

"I get this crap from some rubber ball with tentacles?" TR returned.

"I never thought all your circuits were in use," Z tossed in quickly. "Your ready light's on, but your modem's not connected! You're on constant standby."

"You're putting your mouth in gear before your brain, such as it is, is engaged," Tab replied as quickly. "It's your most endearing quality. Well, it's your closest thing to an endearing quality."

Speaking of quality, I think it's time to recall your model to replace the defective crystals. I liked the modem disconnect thing, Z. It's too bad nobody but the two of us have the least idea what it means.

This would go on for hours. It meant the group was about to start another adventure. They were happy and felt close. The insults and one-upman-ship word games were their tension-breaker and relaxer. They actually had the strongest affection for one another.

"I'll leave before you start shooting," Zianteus said with a chuckle. "Good fortune!"

[We need some!]

Zianteus stepped through the wall and was gone. Thing leaned over to look into Z's eyes.

[Good for you! I was sure you'd say something rude – as usual!]

What's going on?

"Yes, Z," Tab asked. "I saw the look on your face there. What does it mean?"

"Nothing much," Z answered. "It's just a sort of subliminal feeling I have."

[There's a certain logic behind it. Z mentioned it before on Neeneeahna when we were there to answer one of Louahna's previous summonses. Z wondered why she would give us a virtual order to come there. He thinks there's something odd about her attitude. I can see his point.]

"What're you getting at?" TR asked. "I think, just maybe, I have some of the same feelings at times. She tends to act like what the Tendd call a spoiled brat."

"I sometimes wonder if she's started to believe she really is some sort of fairy princess or something," Z answered. "We have to get together to travel across several thousand plazsis (MGS, or Maitan Galactic Standard light years) in ships, using all that time and energy while all she has to do is step onto EC from anywhere in the galaxy, like Zianteus just did – and like both Heleemius and Iaheah have done numerous times.

"She's been here a couple of times. Why have one of them come to tell us to come way the hell over there when she could get here as quickly and easily as they do?"

[It's true. She does seem to make demands when a simple request would serve better. We're all ready to go – in fact, we want to do something. It's the idea there are more considerate ways to handle things.]

Louahna is somewhat self-centered but, as you say, we all want something to do. We each have our own little eccentricities we put up with so one more won't hurt.

[I'm not eccentric! All of you are!]

"You're just plain weird!" TR shot back.

The whole bunch of you are nutzo!

"Did you ever get the major overhaul you were talking about, Maita?" Tab asked. "I think they left some parts out!"

"You and TR were supposed to go in for your billion plazsi checkup," Z said. "I can see you forgot about it – again! You're way overdue for an oil change!"

It wouldn't end before they were on Neeahna.

Chapter one

"We are now in orbit over Neeahna. I'll go aground where we landed before, but I wish they had some designated place for us to land. It would be so much easier that way.*

[She can be to us instantly no matter where we are. That was Z's earlier point.]

That was true. There was no reason to land at any specific spot where the M82nds were concerned – not only in the case of Neeahna. Anywhere in the galaxy.

They landed and were met immediately as they stepped off the ramp.

"I'm glad you came quickly," Louahna greeted. "There seems to be something strange happening on a planet out on the `Q' arm. It's somewhere you've never been before so you'll want to place a new relay station on the way, I'm sure. I should have mentioned that when I sent the message, but you can always run back and pick some up, can't you?

"The coordinates are S one eleven point six, plus two point one four, three fifty four twenty.

"The people are marsupial, nocturnal, cave dwellers. They're intelligent, but not advanced. It seems to me there's some contact with aliens, but I know of no race out there who could be the contacters. It's throwing everything off-center for me. These people have the potential to become a good race and I don't want it ruined."

[Where are the closest space faring races? And what the hell do you mean, `run back?' It's twenty thousand plazsis from here to EC, for the galaxy's sake!]

"The nearest one to Kroop – that's what the people call their world – are at Neal, about two thousand or so plazsis away," Louahna replied, ignoring Thing's second question. I'm sure they haven't gone to Kroop. They wouldn't interfere. Very few races would."

These people are at S three fifty four twenty? That's a hell of a long way out on the arm.

"Yes," Louahna said. "There are thousands of stars out there that we know nothing about. I've been on perhaps two thousand planets in the near area, but that isn't even a fair start. The interlopers could be from anywhere. If they have a drive like your TTH fourteen they could cross the entire galaxy in hours!"

[No one else uses TTH fourteen. Maita or TR can instantly detect anything moving in that plane with ease. Maita has noted broad zi-planal perturbations in only nineteen places and none of them are in close galaxies.]

One's sort of close, in those terms. About a third of the way to M eighty two, but at N plus thirty seven W minus eighty two cast nine on seventeen.

"What the hell was that all about?" Z asked.

"Universal coordinates with this galaxy at its center," Louahna replied. "M eighty two is at N minus twelve E plus two. That's probably the globular cluster galaxy down around there."

She pointed through the planet.

[That's what we figure.]

"Do you mean there are nineteen other galaxies with ships as advanced as Maita?!" Z exclaimed.

"Out of billions of galaxies that's not many," Tab pointed out.

"Oh, crap!" TR exploded. "We don't know if we can detect TTH fourteen in the more distant ones. There may be thousands!

"They're not a high percentage, though. The weakest

signals we receive puts more than seven million galaxies in the sphere, so nineteen is only about point oh oh oh two seven percent. There's certainly no dearth of galaxies with the drive."

[*Dearth*? Great exploding galaxies! Now you're taking up some of Z's snobbery! Heee!]

Thing had been riding on Z's shoulder. Z had suddenly pitched it to Tab, saying, "Here! Hold this! I think it must've dropped out of a tree or something. Have you sprayed for pests recently, Louahna?"

"Hey! That's no reason to get it all over me!" Tab cried, tossing it back.

[Help! These wild *animals* are attacking po' lil ol' defenseless me!]

"They don't need any help," Louahna said. "They seem to be doing a fair job."

Thing pinned Z's arms to his sides by wrapping its tentacles around from behind. [I feel so helpless! Nobody cares if they brutalize pooooor innocent little me!]

"You could maybe use one of those tentacles to cut off his air supply by wrapping it around his neck!" Tab suggested.

[He makes ugly faces and turns a disgusting blue when I do that. He could learn to change into more pleasant hues like the Mord. He shows no consideration at all for anybody!]

Will you two knock it off! We have a job to do!

"Yeah! Knock it off!" Z said. "Thing, that is!"

[Don't you strike me!]

Hold perfectly still, Z. I'll use a heat beam and we can have fried Thing for dinner!

"That's disgusting!" TR snapped. "You know how rubber *smells* when you burn it?"

"Speaking of smells," Tab said. "What kind of oil do you

use on your ramp gears?"

"Rendered Swaz fat!" TR rejoined.

I think I'll have to redesign you two! Tab can look like a rockslug and TR can look like that, what did you call it, Z? Idaho potato?

[Amazing insight! Maita has finally accurately captured your true personalities!]

"At least they *have* personalities!" Z quipped. "Hey! That's about enough!" Thing tightened the tentacles to where Z could barely breathe.

[Say you're sorry and that you'll never insult me again! Say it!]

"Okay!" Z gasped. "Let go!"

Thing released Z and went to his shoulder.

"You crummy little snake!" Z complained. "You almost choked me to death!"

[Hey! You promised never to insult me again! Cheater! Cheater! Oormph root eater!]

"I lied," Z retorted. "Not to mention, I LIKE oormph root!"

Okay! That's enough of that! Please forgive us, Louahna. We've been inactive for so long we're a bit silly. TR, you and Tab go to Kroop and have a look around. We'll go to Neal where we can try to find where any aliens may be who can go to Kroop. They may know of other space faring races Louahna's people may have missed. As she says, there are thousands of worlds out there and there's been very little exploring done in the area.

"I like the way you can play and enjoy each other in these such brutal ways and never take offense," Louahna said. "Maybe this will be something to fill your interests for a little while."

[Just one more thing, Louahna. You almost got into it

yourself. I wasn't sure you understood what we were doing at the time, but I know now! Next time you get your share! You're always fair game when you start it yourself! Be warned!]

Louahna laughed and said, "I was afraid I'd spoken much too soon as it was. I'm not so sure I could come up with retorts quickly enough."

"It takes some getting used to," Tab agreed. "I used to get beaten to slag in the exchanges, but I've learned. We're all very close, but it's not masculine to Z to say he cares about us so we do this as a way to show affection for one another."

That started it again and this time Louahna joined in, but was solidly defeated in almost no time. There was an art to it and one must be most careful not to say anything that could be twisted because that would certainly result in your becoming the center of the remarks.

"I'll do better next time!" she promised as they said their farewells. They rose and headed outward at TTH4 for a short while so they could communicate. It was much more difficult in TTH14 due to the fact 14 was an almost pure-energy plane and interfered with the signals.

They made some plans, then dropped back into N space for Tab to transfer to TR for the trip. They would change from ship to ship as the situation demanded.

They then went back into TTH4, then to TTH14 and were soon at their destination. 14 wasn't accurate to a fine enough degree for navigation so they always made the final several hundred or so plazsis in TTH4.

TR and Tab went to Koop while Maita took Z and Thing to Neal, where they met the large beings there.

The Neals were open and friendly and were happy to meet new peoples from the empire. They were given the fastcom used by the empire and Maita gave them a translator whereby they could talk to the traders guild. (Fastcom carried only printing. It wasn't able to transmit vocals so it was easy to digitalize the Neal language into the translator for the coms. The printer on Neal would automatically translate to Maitan for them and vice versa.) Maita also gave them the schematics and specification for the moder that would allow them to use TTH4 and would put the empire within reach of their own world in a realistic time. They would soon have a flourishing trade with the empire.

The Neals had large droopy ears, wrinkled faces and sad eyes, which caused Z to comment they looked like Bassett hounds from old Earth, though they were really funloving and happy.

Z had learned long ago that looks mean nothing. In some of his first adventures he came across two races, one who resembled cute cuddly Teddy bears and one who looked "mean as hell!"

The Teddy bears were mean as hell while the mean-looking ones were outgoing and friendly – and were willing to risk everything to avoid the possibility of harming another race.

The Neals knew of only two other spacefaring worlds and gave their coordinates to Maita. They were sure neither one would interfere with a developing culture, as they wouldn't. Neither had a good enough drive to visit very much, but the Neals were now hopeful trade would begin in earnest among the "local area" planets as well as with the empire. There were other cultures quite close, relatively, but no one was sure of how safe it would be to cross the space between the galactic arms and the main part of the galaxy. Some very strange things could happen if the theories were correct.

[We crossed and have even been far outside of the galaxy, but we found there's a strong drift factor in the mode we use. It's possible the drift's even stronger in other TTH modes. While the group of empire members and associates are less than ten thousand plazsis away across the break it could be dangerous to go across directly. We can give you the figures and the drift factors if you wish to experiment but I suggest you be most careful. There are stories of test ships that have disappeared for thousands of years. Only we have ever gone outside and returned that we know of and that was a series of accidents we hope most fervently will never happen again to anyone any-where!]

"Is there any reason we would chance the trip there instead of simply going inward on the arm?" the Neals asked.

Z told them of the Zulians, who were located very near the "S" beacon. The Zulians were one of the two races known throughout the entire galaxy for exceptional craftsmanship in every field. They were a funny unclassifiable race who were respected even over the Zeenans for the quality of their work and their products as well as the high quality of the race itself.

They were as known as the Parf for being the finest artists in all fields of art – and the Parf were *indeed* well-known in those fields!

The Zulians were once prepared to allow themselves to become extinct rather than chance that a deadly virus would escape their home world. Maita and the crew barely reached them in time to move them to safety, but that, also, is another story.

Maita then went into orbit where it met with TR and Tab, who could report very little about any contact as they used floaters to collect data. The alternative would be that they make contact themselves, thus compounding the problem.

We have two other space-traveling societies out here. I'll go to Yeel where there's a reptilian society while you go to Oran where there's a Swaz-like race. TR can modify you if you choose, but they should be glad to see us. They're the farthest ones from here. Give them the com setup, a translator and the moder for TTH4. They can join the empire, the traders guild, become associate members or ignore us as it suits them. They don't get moders and junk if they ignore us. I'll flash-relay our experiences with the Neals. You may find something in it to use in the contact with the Oranians.

There was a buzz.

You can see these are a fine people. The coordinates for Oran are in the burst. Meet us at S one forty one, plus one, S two twenty ninety seven in seventy five hours. Good luck.

TR flashed and was gone.

Now for Yeel.

Maita flashed and was gone.

They met the reptilian people on Yeel and were highly impressed they were so easily well-accepted. There were several races in the empire who were much like the Yeel so they voted to become full members of the empire almost immediately.

Z had once marveled at how quickly and easily many cultures immediately gave authority over themselves to the empire and how easily aliens were welcomed among basically different races. He'd learned that once a race had the evolvement and intelligence to develop the IDmode drives that opened up space to them they knew there was nothing but good to come from other races who had done the same. Any damage to a race had generally been the result of good intentions in the wrong place at the wrong time. Premature contact with a race could be devastating to that race. It could, in fact, destroy the chance for race to ever evolve socially or to become anything at all. It could result in a resentment and the feeling that more advanced societies were condescending to them.

The empire was primarily a coordinating machine to a galaxywide trading guild. Even the poorest planet had something that was needed elsewhere, so all prospered. The empire would emplace the guild machines that handle all laws and government duties to eliminate almost all the incredible bureaucracies built up over a period of time. Maita and crew slowly learned during their far-ranging explorations that more growing civilizations had fallen due to those exponential increases in obstructive bureaucracies than from all their wars combined. Nothing was more devastating to a society than a deep sense of frustration and hopelessness – and bureaucrats fed on exactly those things. The old Kheth Federation, large and powerful as it had been, had been on the verge of falling back into barbarism because of the bureaucracies. Being the first outside petitioner to join the Maitan Empire was the only thing that saved them from ruin and primitivization of the multiculture there. No one was required to accept what the machines said, but most did. It was more efficient and saved vast sums of both time and monetary administration costs. A machine could give a decision in picoseconds most times and one machine would replace hundred buildings full of bureaucrats.

A machine was just in legal questions so most used them with any added mitigation questions handled by an organic judge to be appointed by the governed. The machines had mental probes built in one could use by choice (But there was no coercion except in the case of capital crimes where a convicted person could be put under the probe. The reasoning was that as the subject was under sentence of death the probe could save that person. He had life to gain and nothing to lose) as that could settle a question of guilt or innocence finally and fully. It was impossible for an organic mind to lie to the machines.

The information the machine extracted was available to no one except for the questions agreed upon beforehand – again except in capital cases where others involved could be shown.

It wasn't possible to lie to the probe because it read the mind directly, meaning that it could establish innocence immediately.

There was no stigma to refusing the machine. Many people of many races simply would not trust their fate to a machine. The machines left on the worlds carried needed information to and from Hospital, Library and emergency response agencies such as Fleet and the various "local" police agencies and could summon empire help, particularly the highest priority data, medical, instantly.

All science and history, medical knowledge and/or anything else needed was immediately available through either Library or Hospital. Emperor Maita could be reached directly through coding EC3000 on any fastcom or the machines. Library would transfer unanswered questions directly to University upon request.

Some worlds had restricted use of the machines because they had not yet earned certain things for themselves. Handing a race everything it could want or need before it matured enough to use the information properly could rob future generation of pride of accomplishment, which was another thing that could devastate a race.

That was another thing that must be considered at the time of placement. There are some things that must be earned to have real meaning.

After their stay on Yeel they decided to look over a near-by planet with floaters as they had a few hours before they were expected to meet with Tab and TR.

The Yeel gave me the nav coordinates for a world they call Baken. The people are reptiles, but are very birdlike, carrying the vicious traits some birds seem to have. They aren't expected to survive to a much more advanced state because of their extreme territorial instinct and excessive aggressiveness. The Yeel were certainly glad to get the empire's coordinate system! I had to translate these coordinates (The screen showed s341.98732 A~<jJ 22KR 56.34211F 34389B 2121.34L45~8F ssTw2swe4776.7D E112F3 Yeel system = S139/0/S22866 in Maitan Galactic Standard). I gave them new moders and signaling system and fastcom. Now they can go almost anywhere. They have several things that will bring the traders out here. Here's Baken.

The planet was a bit barren in some places, but was also a pleasant-seeming place in others. The Baken didn't congregate closely and it was more than obvious from the spy floater scans that population pressure was already pushing them too close so there would be a bloody time soon. There was nothing they could do to prevent it so they made scan reports for Library, then returned to compare notes with Tab and TR.

"There's a pleasant planet called Ial in quite close to Elit and Exit with another highly intelligent culture," TR reported. "The Oranians visit them often because they like them.

The Oranians are amphibious and can get along quite well with an aquatic culture, which the Ials are. They resemble the porpoise of Earth or the Zeezians.

"I had some time so I visited. I found them to be fun.

"There's a planet with a transfer station on it established by the Oranians. I placed a relay nearby and visited with the crew at the station. The planet's called Feef and is a rock a lot like Ape's World was when you first found it. They've recently begun planoforming it and another world halfway between Oran and Neal they call Zirst. They want to share Zirst with Neal as a training station. They've joined the empire and have the TTH four drive, but they said they like the challenges and are learning a lot so they'll continue the planoformings. It'll save half the time of travel between the worlds and they can put an empire traders guild transfer station on it. It's central to this galactic arm so it'll be viable for all those reasons and more.

"I guess you can see I liked the people.

"Here's a data complete. You can give me a complete of your activities."

There was a buzz for several seconds as Maita sent the new information it had gathered. TR and Maita shared most forms of information so either could act as backup for the other in case some freak accident, attack or sabo-tage deprogrammed any of the comps in either of them.

We can meet on Zirst. I would very much like to see that work in progress and could report about it to Vendu and Searcher (An intelligent planoforming station). The MGS coordinates are S one thirty four minus two S twenty seven four oh one?

"Yo!" TR answered. "I think the best thing we did for those people was to give them a usable coordinate system. What did you think of the one they were using?"

It was a monster! I'll see you at Zirst. Last one there's a rockslug!

Maita and TR flashed into IDmode drive almost simultaneously but, due to the extreme TTH14 inconsistency, were far apart on breaking back into N space. They met above Zirst and landed not far from the dome of the planoforming project. Maita sent Thing and Z in on floaters to inspect progress of the operation. Z made a few suggestions gleaned from his experiences on Ape's World. He liked the people as much as Tab did.

Maita always used the floaters to communicate with others, explaining that the emperor must always remain isolated in the ship by law. When it was necessary for the emperor to appear, which was almost never, Z or Tab were disguised to handle it. It wasn't likely the empire would long survive the knowledge the emperor was a machine yet. Too many people would resist the idea, would soon break away, trade would become overly competitive and uncontrolled, wars might start among the more primitive members and chaos would reign.

Maita didn't like being emperor, but was originally designed for the job so had a fatalistic attitude about it. The ruling was programmed in by the original Maitans more than two thousand years ago so Maita accepted what fate had thrown to it. They were, both Maita and the others in the crew, pleased that those sophisticated machines did almost all the actual running of the empire, leaving Maita free to adventure with them.

As Maita often said, it could be destroyed on one of their little jaunts and it would, barring any extreme emergency, be many thousands of years before anyone ever knew!

Later when they were all in orbit again Z and Thing were in the pilot's dome on Maita where there was a special chair that was infinitely adjustable. Z had claimed it as his own more than ninety years ago. Thing was curled into a ball in his lap and they were in contact with Tab and TR through the holovid screen.

"We seem to have reached a dead end so far," Tab reported. "We've gotten some new members to enter the empire, but we still have no idea where the problem at Kroop originates. I hope someone has a plan?"

[Let's go to Kroop and start a search pattern. We can scan for com radiations all over the area. They're almost to the end of the arm so we can go out and work inward. I want to know if the damage to one primitive planet is worth all this ridiculous effort. Louahna may have greatly overreacted and they couldn't pose a threat anyhow.]

Not if it would stop there. We have to meet them and make it plain that kind of interference won't be tolerated. It's far too dangerous to the future of the empire. Look at what happened to the Immins!

[I would prefer never to hear the word `Immin' again so long as the omniverse exists.]

"Wouldn't we all!" Z agreed. "On the other hand, if we can prevent something like that from being repeated it's worth any effort. It'll take those scars centuries to heal."

"We'll scan every planet that broadcasts any form of distant communications," Tab suggested. "We've found space faring races with no more than radio.

"TR and I'll take from the tip toward galactic edge and you take toward galactic center, okay?"

That's fine with me. Let's get started, TR.

"Yo!" TR replied.

They both flashed and were gone.

They did visual scans for a number of planets and came

on one with elementary radio. Radio was generally used for a relatively short time in most cultures' development, they could determine with fair accuracy what to expect in technology.

Steam to intrasystem rocket space travel.

I've analyzed the language and it makes no sense whatever. We'll go in and have a look.

The planet was dubbed Mine (MEE nuh), the Maitan word for unusual and was listed at S110/-1/S36860. It was an entirely pleasant place with many settlements that seemed to be gathered near lodes of minerals. Maita sent floaters to scan.

*I can see why the language made no sense! We have no common basis. The people are intelligent plants! They're dome-shaped with ten pairs of short legs and several smaller arms with hands of four fingers. They contain chlorophyll and congregate around mineral deposits their physiologies can use. *They* aren't our villains here! If anything was ever certain, that is!*

[We must use the spy floaters to scan for awhile! This is a discovery that makes the trip worthwhile if we find nothing else at all! I must ask Louahna if they contact these races, though I doubt it. They wouldn't have any basis for understanding.]

They stayed a few hours while the floaters brought material for Thing's studies. There was a huge datacube library begun.

The next occupied planet they visited was called Altry by the natives, who were in the fossil fuel age and had radio and television. Maita used that to gather information about the people and the society.

They're mammals, L-type, two meters or less, furry and slow moving. The planet's much too warm for much exertion. They aren't advanced enough to be our target.

They were prepared to move when TR called to say, "I think I've found it."

Report.

"I'll send everything," TR replied. There was the buzz of intense modem download (One of Z's terms).

TR has gone to a planet called Lemp, which is way out toward the end of the arm. There are reptiles in primitive farming communities. Next, it was a planet called Uhly, which is close in that vicinity and is peopled by equally primitive mammals. There are radio senders above both planets is why TR went there. The next planet is radiating a number of different bands in the com ranges and is called Sear. It seems it could be our target world. They've apparently invented some kind of drive by accident. The nature of the radios above the other two planets suggests they were placed there by the Searians. We are here.

[No kidding?! I thought we were somewhere else!]

Don't start. We'll dock with TR to figure our next move.

They were above the atmosphere of an M3 type world tending toward M2 configuration, which means it was much like planets such as Zeena, Mome-Ah, Terra and Feach, but tended toward the cooler and more austere end of the spectrum. TR met them and they conferred about the best way to handle things.

I'll just land and demand some explanations! They aren't advanced enough to where they won't react to my size and visible external appendages. Hold on.

[I think it would be a mistake to start making demands based only on unstudied assumptions, Maita.]

Why?

"We don't do things that way, Maita! Come on!" Tab

cried. "We don't know what's going on and we don't come on like some kind of bully! Not ever! What's the matter with you?"

I basically wanted to bait you into a response like that and I really don't have any plan yet. Now it's up to YOU to make the plan!

"You seemed to react pretty strongly, even so, Maita," Z said. "What's on your mind about this place?"

Ever since Immins were mentioned I've been worried. These people have a drive they shouldn't have and are putting satellites around planets whose broadcasts won't reach this place for a thousand years! Where did they get that drive? It's exactly the kind of thing Immins would do! Do you know what I'll do if I find any damned Immins out here? Do you think I could continue with any facade of sanity if we keep finding those – I won't say it! – every-where we go?

[No way. Not Immins. Forget them out here. We're up against something very strange here, but Immins aren't it. It's something stranger than that. It may be some such society just beginning, but I feel such a society would never find stellar travel on their own. Not a TTH drive. They would use science to destroy themselves.]

"I agree," Tab said.

"Me too. No Immins or even anything much like them in this place," TR added.

"Let's do land, Maita. We can talk it over with someone. Find out what the deal is," Z suggested. "I don't think this one's too serious, but I could be wrong."

[Wrong?! You?! Never! Oh, gasp and gurgle! I am shocked! This is terrible! Must I be left with *nothing* to believe in? Heeee!]

Z picked Thing up and tossed it into the air, but it reached around his neck with a tentacle and swung around to drop behind him where it was able to pin his arms.

You two don't start. We're landing.

[With consent?]

Yeah. Radio.

They sat at a large space port pad area and TR soon sat next to them. Maita shielded, but no attack came. Shortly an electric cart came out with four beings on it. They weren't armed. Z studied them on the holovid screen as they came to Maita's ramp. They were reptilian, somewhat shorter than he was and seemed very quick-moving. They had tan leathery skin, slightly flattened heads and protuberant eyes.

"C'mon, Thing," he said. "Let's go invite them in."

Thing climbed onto his shoulder. They went to room one and out onto the loading ramp. They had used digital radio to get landing instructions so now would have to get someone to use the probe to extract language.

The four Searians were chattering animatedly among themselves and seemed extremely curious about Thing, who managed to get across to them they needed someone to put on a headgear so they could extract the language.

Over the years the crew had learned through meetings with thousands of people from many hundreds of worlds the easiest way to begin communication without language was with signs. The process was improved enough to where they were able to quickly get one of the Searians to volunteer to use the probe. Within half an hour Z had a crystal to place in his earlobe socket that gave him full use of the language and knowledge of the Searian culture.

"I'm called Z. This is Thing. That's Tab coming from the other ship and this ship is called Maita," Z announced in the Searian language. "The ship Tab left is called TR. The floater just overhead is a communications device through which you may speak to Maita and through which Maita and Thing will speak to you. Thing is an empath and can't vocalize without the help of machines.

"May I invite you inside?"

The Searians conferred among themselves, then one stepped forward.

"I am called Noam. I am female, which is not so visible a thing among us as it is among you mammals," she said. "This is Creem, male, Lot, male and Quad, female. We are curious about you and your ships. We would like to enter."

They went in and to room two, the meeting, instruction and medical room.

"Please take a comfortable bench and be seated if you wish," Z invited. "We've traced you here from the radio sources you placed around Lemp and Uhly and wish to know their purpose."

"Their purpose?" Creem asked. "They're information gathering devices. They tell us about many weather and geological features of the planets."

[But it will be a thousand years before the information reaches here if it doesn't all damp out long before it gets this far. What's the point?]

The Searians looked puzzled.

That was Thing. It uses stupid idioms that don't make sense. I use this tone when I speak. I am Maita, the ship.

Z grinned at that. The reference was to the fact he had used idioms none of them understood for years after they first were brought together. Thing had always made fun of the terms.

"The ship is intelligent?" Quad asked.

"Yes," Tab answered. "So is my ship, TR. Our ships are our friends and partners as well as our conveyances."

"We met an intelligent machine," Noam said. "It gave us the drive for our ships. It was a very sad machine."

We represent a large empire toward galactic center. I very much wish to meet this machine. Do you know where it was heading?

"It has gone into intergalactic space," Lot replied. "It said it was.... But you can see the recordings it left for us. It was so sad!

"May we see other parts of you, Maita?"

Most certainly! Show these people around, Z. We can then go to where the recordings are kept. I'm very curious about such a machine. Why would it go into intergalactic space? That's almost suicidal! Something is very wrong here!

"Its makers died in a catastrophe so it gave us the drive because we are so much like them," Creem explained.

Z showed them all around Maita and they didn't seem at all surprised there were so few aboard a ship sixty meters across. They were delighted by the elevators and the pilot's dome, which was on the bottom of the ship and had its own gravity, allowing passengers to walk "upside-down" with the ground only a few meters "under" their heads.

The elevator rotated as it came to the dome or one would find himself with his head at the floor. The Searians didn't yet have artificial gravity and enjoyed the novelty of walking upside down.

They soon returned to the outside where Z, Tab and Thing (On its floater) accompanied the Searians to a building, then to a larger building in the nearby large city where they were shown the recordings from the machine who gave them the drive. The ship was of the "needle" type, designed and built by a reptilian race of people. They developed TTH1 mode drive when someone discovered the omniversal theory before they discovered the relativity theory, therefore passing over years of dead-end theoretical work. They had built and programmed the ship, given it their most advanced computerization and used it only a few years before a plague wiped them out. The ship had been wandering for about three hundred years before it met the Searians. It determined they were a worthwhile race who closely resembled its builders, both physically and psychologically. It gave them the secrets of the drive, instructed them in the ways of space travel, then set off for the next galaxy. It felt itself to be without purpose so was going to try to meet people in another galaxy where so many things might be different.

"In TTH one it won't reach another galaxy for more than six thousand years – and that without the drift factor," Tab said.

[It's a truly brave and wonderful machine! It shouldn't have interfered with these people, but there's little or no evidence any harm has yet come of it. What can we do?]

"How long ago was it here?" TR asked through Tab.

"The ship left six years ago," Noam answered. "I can get the actual date. It said it was going toward the galaxy we call `The Tlurf Tail' to our galactic north."

What's your idea, TR?

"If I know exactly how long ago it left and exactly where it planned to go I can use fourteen to intercept it and get it to come back. We know we can travel in TTH one in intergalactic space and it won't be too far," TR replied.

"Wouldn't drift make it impossible to find?" Z asked.

[The drift would tend to balance in TTH one and fourteen over this amount of time to a direct, calculable ratio. TR could be there in sixty three or four hours, but it would take such a ship at least six years to get back to this galaxy and perhaps a year to get back here after the return because drift will carry it away toward galactic east.]

"Why would it want to return?" Z asked.

*It's terribly alone and is in terrible pain. These people could put it to use and could become actual friends to it. If not them the Zulians could certainly find a use that would be good both for it *and* for them! It's programmed to go on. You know my feelings about that. It's hundreds of years old and is terribly sad. It has no way to end its terrible pain. It's a wonderful thing it isn't insane!*

"Tab and Maita, let's collect every scrap information we can about that ship," TR said. "Thing can help with the math. Maybe I can reach it and bring it back home."

"You aren't serious!" Z cried. "You can't go that far from the galactic edge! You couldn't get back!"

[It isn't really impossible. We've all left the galaxy for short distances. That ship isn't close to halfway point yet so there's plenty of time.]

"You're crazy!" Z said.

No one asked you for any help. You don't have to go.

"Like bloody hell! I'm just as crazy as you are! You go and I go!" Z replied. "I know very well we will. That's how we are and none of us would have it any other way."

"No one goes but me," TR stated. "It's high risk, but Maita can always make another ship. No one could make another Maita or another of you organics. This is all theoretical, anyhow."

I won't waste my time arguing because I know you're right. I doubt that anyone will go. The math will be too difficult even for Thing. By the time we have it worked out the ship could be too far to dare to go after. Let's finish here and allow Thing and TR to work on the math without any outside distractions. I see some truly fascinating possibilities!

The Searians gave them all the information they had at their disposal while Z and Tab explored the planet a bit and Thing, TR and Maita worked on the planal math. Tab was in constant gravitic communication through his internal contacts with TR. Z met with the Lead Council of Searian Scientists and held discussions about contacting other races who may be harmed. He played a couple hours of the records of the Immins, which was a truly excellent way to show a worst-case scenario – and it was all fact. By the time Maita was through with the intergalactic space problem Z had agreements with the Searians. They joined the empire and were ready to receive fastcom and TTH4 moders for their ships.

The Searians had made no contacts with other races yet. They had only put out the recording and radio broadcast senders, so no damage was done. The senders sent to passive recorders at the outskirts of the solar systems that were to be collected at fixed intervals, meaning it was unnecessary for them to physically enter the systems once the satellites were placed.

"That means this isn't the problem world we're looking for out here," Z explained to Maita and the crew. "The Searians haven't done anything to get Louahna's attention.

"We've barely started our search. This was only a side trip.

"The Searians are a bit hyper, but I pretty much like them."

[What the hell is hyper? You sound as bad as Maita when Maita's trying to sound as bad as you!]

"*You're* the one who used Z's idioms with these people!" TR snapped.

"They move a lot – fast, or rather, quick," Z explained.

"They talk a lot. They ask a lot of questions and they're amazingly curious."

Z means they appear hyperactive, physically as well as psychologically.

"You'll have to finish the search while TR and I go out," Tab said.

"You're *going*?!" Z cried.

[They have a fifty-fifty chance of finding something, which is a heck of a lot better odds than we usually operate under. Their chance of returning is almost one hundred percent. They can visual, then follow the nav beacons from anywhere in the galaxy. Coming back is easier than going.]

Z shook his head. "You guys aren't going to listen to me so I'll just say please be careful. We need you."

They most definitely will. I've modified some circuits to make two extra layers of checks and balances and added another failsafe system. If they run into any situation where there's even very serious doubt they return. Automatically.

[In addition we're going to re-re-recheck every possible contingency and we're drilling through the mathematical sequence again. I'm going to throw variables at them as fast as I can think of them. If anything comes up that we can't solve they don't go anywhere.]

They spent more time studying the math while Maita placed two fastcom relays so they could communicate from any part of the galactic arm.

"Maita's ordered several new fastcom sets from New Zule to replace what we'll use here," TR said. "They're ready and I'm going after them. I'll jump the space between the arm and the galactic central area toward New Zule. I can calibrate for the drift and any unexpected factors. It'll be good experience. I'll also pause between jumps to check everything as I go. We've been a lot farther out into intergalactic space than that, but this time I won't be in a panic to get back.

"I'll also be using TTH fourteen instead of TTH one so I can figure exactly what's happening and can compare it to our present equations."

[Go for it! I want the best recordings you've ever made of everything that happens. I'll run complete recalibration sequences for every trip we've ever made in fourteen and can cross-reference to find the exponential ratios on the J factor, which should give us a twist-drift constant we can use with any trip we made in TTH fourteen. The trip in will give a direct reverse ratio to the trip out as the drift factor decreases at the circumference. Factor that with the twist-drift and we should have something we can use from now on. We will be able to figure intragalactic trips to a much closer destination point.]

"Yo! We go!" TR said and was gone.

While TR was gone Maita replaced all the relay setups on the Searians' satellites orbiting Lemp and Uhly to send them fastcom instead of radio. It used pulses at wide intervals so didn't use much energy plus they would get information at Sear immediately. They allowed the four original Searians they met to accompany them out as well as two other Searians whose job it would be to service the fastcoms in case of trouble (Trouble? With a *Zulian* set? Not in *your* lifetime! Get real!) They were amazed by Maita's drive.

The crew was sure they would be a positive force in the empire, though they were among the ten least advanced races with full membership. They were curious, highly intelligent and honest.

They returned to await TR's return. It was already more than a day late, but Maita was in contact while it was at New Zule so knew there was a delay. That didn't lessen Z's nervousness and Maita threatened to sedate him. When TR was back it explained it had merely stopped to recalibrate everything at New Zule, then had fine-tuned everything again en route back, which took time. The whole process was much safer as a result.

"I've bettered my odds to sixty five to thirty five now," TR reported. "I also learned some things about the drift. If it's a direct ratio out there like I think it'll be I've got it made as to coming and going. My only real problem is going to be in locating the ship once I get out there. It didn't have fastcom.I've figured it as close as I can if I leave at zero o'clock ship's time tomorrow night.

"Does that suit everyone? Tab?"

"Yo!" Tab replied. "I'm anxious to get started.

"How do you know where it was headed?"

"Working from what it told the Searians," TR replied.

Yes. We'll all be extremely nervous until we hear your return transmission. We'll spend the remaining time together tomorrow evening until your launch.

They spent the rest of the day and the following helping the Searians emplacing the TTH4 moders Maita manufactured into the four ships the Searians had. All traders with the empire and of the empire had the drive so the Searians would have to trade for any moders in the future.

An empire station was placed and Sear was an active trader of the Maitan Empire Traders Guild before the time for TR and Tab to try the experiment of going after the alien ship.

When the time came Maita accompanied TR to the edge of the arm where the crew watched as it made the jump.

"I understand why TR had to go after the machine," Z said. "I know how you feel about manufacturing an intelligent entity who has no choice about existence and I know that machine's in pain and feels absolutely alone.

"I'm worried about TR and Tab going outside the galaxy and will keep worrying until they're back.

"I wonder why it didn't occur to the machine that it could become the friend of the Searians and could end its loneliness that way?"

*It isn't psychologically prepared to be the ship with these amazing people. I think its makers were a truly fine race who the Searians *too* much resemble. I'll want it to go on to New Zule to become a friend and partner with the Zulians. I'll also want to introduce it to Maita Searcher (an intelligent planoforming machine). We can give it both machine companionship and organic. The Zulians are the finest people the galaxy's ever known and their history with that virus almost destroying them gives a strong basis for understanding. TR, Searcher and I will give it our psychological support.*

[The machine was designed to be an explorer and an opener of new fields of science to its makers. The makers are no more, but it can be fulfilled by working as that very explorer for the Zulians. The Zulians will also be true friends to the machine so both will profit greatly from the relationship.]

It's one of those odd accidents of fate that it took this arm instead of the next. It might have found the Zulians itself, that way.

"It only has radio. No fastcom," Z pointed out. "It isn't too likely it would've found anything except these rather primitive cultures. I wish we could've found its builders before their plague wiped them out."

It was long ago. The Pweetoos were running their empire clear across the galaxy from here. No one had left the empire yet.

[It's a pity we weren't around then. I hope we can help the machine. I want to know more about its makers. Are we going back to Sear?]

"What for?" Z asked.

[To await TR's return.]

It will be quite some time at best and I would be insane with worry if we weren't doing something to fill the time. We've searched only twelve planets so far and haven't found what we're looking for so it's best we continue. I'm sure you'll prefer that to sitting around waiting. I have the empire business to occupy some of my time. You must have something to do even more than I.

"You know that!" Z exclaimed. "You'd have me to bury before ten days were up! I'd die of worry. I'm already more hyper than the Searians."

[I hoped you'd want to work. I'd be in as bad a shape if we were to become inactive now. You're getting to me through the empathy and adding to my own trepidations. Do we have any plan we can follow?]

We have a definite plan. We'll go ahead with the search pattern we're already in and try to locate something. We'll decide what to do if we find anything.

[That's a plan?]

"Face it, Thing. It's more of a plan than most of the things we do!" Z pointed out.

Looking at it logically, we have far more chance of disaster than TR!

[Logic? Us? Get real!]

They called Sear on the new fastcom to explain that they would continue on with their mission.

They found a planet with primitive radio not far from Sear (As those things go in galactic rel-distances) that called itself Zrop. It was peopled by an unclassifiable lifeform. The crew made no contact. The people weren't far enough advanced.

Next they found another very strange one. It had more advanced communications and was called Nex. The people were intelligent plants who would never be able to leave the overly-specialized conditions of that planet so they made no contact.

[This is something that's always intrigued me: the way things seem to happen in bunches. We've been exploring around for almost a hundred years over most of the galaxy and never found any intelligent plants anywhere before. Now we find two planets full of them in just a few ship days and in a narrow part of the galaxy!]

"We've all noticed those kinds of things," Z agreed. "On Earth we always said things happen in threes."

Horse, as you would say on Earth, manure!

The next world was even more advanced. It was called Grodd by the people, a mammalian species much like the Bentans in the empire. (All the recent planets they explored were on or close to the 0 level because Maita was following the rim of the arm. There were a series of stars in the near area that were likely to have produced more advanced lifeforms.)

Grodd was an M3 normal world and was second from the star in a family of nine planets. It had two fairly large moons, was a bit more than three fifths water-covered and the largest part of the world was in tropical and temperate temperature zones. There were many varieties of life shown on the scanners.

"Maita?"

Yes?

"Why do planets with big moons have so much more variety in lifeforms than those with no moons or only little ones? I've noticed that for years."

Gravity.

"What do you mean?"

[The gravity fields of the larger moons stir the oceans when the organic compounds are being formed early in evolution. That results in a great many more combinations in the original genetic strings, which results in more mutations and hybrids. The same currents disperse the life that forms more widely so it's more likely to end in a spot where it's viable.]

I think maybe we've found our problem planet here! They have several protective satellites. They don't have a fastcom that can be used except from high energy stations so we have a situation much like the old empire before the Federation contact.

"Let's go in. We'll never know sooner," Z said.

[Yes. It will give us something to do and they might even want to fight us! That'll distract our minds! Isn't it strange I want someone to attack you just to divert my own thoughts from worry? Maybe I should get in the medical box for an overhaul!]

"I hope there's some crazy weird kind of puzzle out here or something really odd," Z agreed. "Anything to make me concentrate on something ... outside. Even a natural catastrophe would be nice.

"Listen to *me* now! And you said *you* might need an overhaul, Thing?"

My whole damned crew has been exposed to too much radiation or something! I was a fool to allow TR to go out there like that! I can't stand much more of this! We have to hear from TR. Nothing else is going to do it. I want to know how well our math works and I want to know Tab and TR are sitting out there laughing at us! I'm going in with scanner-floaters to survey the whole damned planet. Maybe we can find what's going on out here, straighten them out and go just off the galactic rim to wait. This keeping busy thing isn't working worth a damn!

[You can say that again! I only wish we had some method to communicate. TR could tell us how stupid we are and we could relax.]

"You two don't go over the edge on me!" Z cried. "*I'm* the one who does things like that!"

Their hearts (Or other components) were no longer in what they were doing. They had been outside the galactic current whirlpool before and knew the dangers. They had a job to do. They would do it. That didn't stop the worry.

Chapter two

They orbited the planet for about seven hours while their scanners went to the surface to gather information. They were able to get the three major languages, locate the main areas of industrialization and military bases and learn a good amount about present problems and news from the television transmissions they monitored.

They don't have much more advancement than television and don't use fastcom. That's a strange thing about cultures on this arm so far. No fastcom.

[They might only have the energy-inefficient type you had a hundred twenty five years ago and can't use it as a portable com because of lack of sufficient power to drive it. Remember, it was only when you combined the Maitan fastcom with the federation system that you got the easy-to-use system you have now.]

I do tend to forget sometimes how far along the theories must be before the efficient types are even possible to a race. I also remember your remarks about synergic scientific development.

"I don't see why they haven't seen us, what with all their satellites and machines," Z said. "You'd think they'd say or do something."

Oh, they've seen us. They're just waiting to see what we're going to do.

"Hmmm. What do you know about them from the TV?" Z asked.

[They're K-type mammals much like the Bentans, but seem somewhat more advanced than Bentans were when they were first contacted. They tend to be more aggressive than many cultures at this stage of development, but they haven't had any modifying contacts. There's far more contact in other areas of space – so far.]

"What do we do?" Z asked.

I could radio them for landing instructions. We could say we were waiting here while our translator machines decoded their language so we could make contact. They have no reason to question that. They don't seem overly worried about us as it is!

"I'll go along with that suggestion," Z replied. "We can try to establish exactly what kinds of problems they're making on Louahna's worlds."

[I agree. Have you heard anything from TR?]

Too soon. I'm in contact with Grodd. It seems to be causing quite a stir down there. They were only waiting for us to say or do something before they did anything. Strange.

It took about half an hour for the Groddians to give them landing instructions, then Maita settled on the space port area they requested. The ship took up the entire space available.

It seems they couldn't agree which country was to handle the problem of the primary contact with us. It could be a real boon or a real disaster and they aren't diplomatically prepared. They're very nervous about it. They knew it would happen sooner or later, but everyone always thought it would be much later so they didn't plan anything for when it happened.

"Surely they didn't believe they were the only planet with spaceflight!" Z said. "The fact they developed it and found other cultures would show them later contacts were likely and sooner ones very possible!"

[It doesn't seem to be a sort of thing they've considered seriously. I hope they aren't like the Kroon. That would explain their willingness to interfere with less advanced cultures. I don't think I could put up with a bunch of hypocritical, pious, sanctimonious pains in the ass right now – and I don't even have an ass for them to be a pain in!]

They don't seem able to decide whether they should meet us armed or unarmed.

"I'll go out on the rim and wait," Z suggested. "I won't be carrying anything so they may decide we're not going to blow them away without provocation."

[*Must* you use those expressions? Blow them away? You are so crass!]

Don't you two start. We're all tense, but it's because we worry like mother hens, as Z says, about Tab and TR, not because of these people. Undress except for a loincloth or something. They have near nudity on their television so they shouldn't be shocked by your general lack of taste.

[Don't start us two? What about you? Who the hell do you think you are – anyhow?]

"Maita makes the rules. It doesn't follow them."

They sparred with words a few minutes, then Z went out onto the rim. Thing didn't go yet because Z wanted to start with something not quite so totally alien. He sat on the edge of the ramp with his feet hanging over and waited. Soon two Groddians came nervously to him in an electric cart that reminded Z of a golf cart from Earth. They stopped and fidgeted a moment, then one got off the cart to approach.

"Uh, I am Keenan, director of extra-Groddian affairs," he said. "Welcome to Grodd."

Z grinned and said, "I'm Z, representative from the Maitan Empire. It's mostly toward galactic center from here. I know how nervous you probably feel right now because we're the first advanced beings you've met, but you'll find most races get along very well with their contacts. I've got quite a lot of experience with contacts so I'll make suggestions if you don't mind."

"Uh, well, uh, certainly. I admit to being at a loss as to how to proceed," Keenan replied.

"Maita, lower the ramp please," Z requested, then suggested to Keenan, "You can come into the ship to meet with us or I can come to your offices – whichever you prefer.

"There's a being inside who you'll find to be totally alien, but it's a member of what's probably the most intelligent race in the galaxy, so don't be surprised.

"The ship is called Maita. It's our project leader as well as our friend and partner."

"The ship? Your project leader and partner?!" Keenan exclaimed. "I don't understand! How can a ship...? I don't understand?"

"Don't understand what?" Z asked.

"The ship is a machine!" the second Groddian cried as he came to the ramp.

"Certainly," Z replied. "We haven't yet met an organic being who can travel space without a ship – well, except the M Eighty Seconds – and they're *part* machine."

"Machine intelligences have been postulated here, but only in fiction," Keenan explained. "My aide here is called Donart."

"There are machine societies," Z replied as they entered the ship. He led them to room two where Thing was seated on a bench by the main console studying the screen. They stared wide-eyed at it as Z introduced them.

"This is Thing, the empath I was telling you about. It can speak through the speakers Maita uses. Maita's the ship's designation if you want to say anything or ask it a question.

"So you'll know which is speaking I'll have both Maita and Thing say something for you. Note the tones and you won't be confused as to who's speaking at a given time.

"Maita? Thing? If you'll please introduce yourselves?"

I am Maita, the ship.

[I am Thing, the fabulously intelligent being about whom Z recently spoke.]

"Don't let it swell your head too much!" Z snapped. "I'd hate to have to clean up what the results of *that* explosion would be off the walls!"

[Hah! You're just jealous because I'm so much more attractive than you are!]

To what? One of Z's octopuses?

[Octopi.]

"An octopus is an animal with eight tentacles. It's native to my home planet," Z said. "Thing's always been jealous of them."

The two Groddians were staring about looking for the exit.

Don't worry about us. We play and joke. Your own television has many comedy shows so we feel little inhibition. We have rather strange senses of humor. You'll get used to us, I suppose. To me, anyhow. One can explain some things, but one may find others aren't quite so easily defined. I would define Z as a pompous ass and Thing as a Mentan mental case!

"Uh, I see," Keenan said. "Er, how did you find us?"

"We landed here and you found us!" Z replied.

Keenan stared at him.

[We were called to this area because you're interfering with developing cultures. That's a mistake some newly advanced races make. It must stop. It can eventually cause unimaginable damage to those races.]

"What do you mean?" Donart asked. "I don't understand most of what is happening here or what you're saying."

It's a thing that can get you into unbelievable trouble later. Untraveled societies seldom realize the damage they're causing or how serious the thing can become. We could tell you stories you wouldn't believe – and they're true!

"But we haven't ever interfered with anyone!" Keenan cried. "We have laws against it!"

[Oh, great exploding galaxies! What's going on here? This is getting too crazy even for *us*!]

"Tell us about those laws," Z requested. "I think maybe we're the ones who don't understand."

"We may contact no people. We must wait for them to contact us," Keenan answered. "We don't know how aggressive strangers may be so we may do nothing unless they institute the contact, then we must proceed with extreme caution."

[Whoo, boy! Our progress here's strictly in reverse!]

They stayed for three days on Grodd and found the Groddians were, indeed, not the ones who were causing the trouble. They hadn't contacted any race as they feared they weren't ready themselves for the contact or trade. It was to be the decision of others entirely.

Maita and crew were then spaceborne again.

I assume we keep looking?

"Why not?" Z replied. "We haven't found what we're looking for.

"Any word from our intrepid partners yet?"

No.

They found two more planets with emerging lifeforms, but not advanced enough to be part of the problem.

"Maita?" Z said the next ship's day.

Yes, Z?

"Let's go to Neeahna. There's something big missing here," Z suggested. "I get the feeling there's something she deliberately hasn't told us or something."

[I agree. I'm slowly beginning to become rather suspicious of her motives as Z's been all along. I wish I knew why!]

We're on our way. I agree, too, not so much about Louahna's personality, but that there's something we haven't been told or that we've missed. We have to discover what it is and we have to resolve it. We can't progress at this rate.

When they arrived on Neeahna no one was there so they went to Neeneeahna. Heleemius went after Louahna. It was almost an immediate thing as they simply "stepped" from place to place.

"What's the emergency?" Louahna asked.

We've found sixteen planets without locating our villain. We've added some to the empire and even found two worlds with intelligent plantlife forms, a very rare thing. We found a ship had been to Sear that then left for intergalactic space. Its makers died out from a plague and it was lonely and grieving. It gave the Searians the drive, then left. Tab and TR have gone after it to try to convince it to return. We want to introduce it to Searcher and to have it become a friend and ally with the Zulians. We found another spacetraveling race who feel they're as yet unprepared for strong contact, but they won't long delay the use of the traders guild. This isn't important. We need more information if we're to find the solution to your problem. We could spend too many years on the type of search we're presently employing here. It's somewhat interesting but, until Tab and TR are back our nerves won't stand the routine day after day. There must be something you can tell us to speed this thing up for us. We simply don't have time to search the arm for the next hundred years when we have no idea what we're looking for!

"I know how you feel about any ship that can't end a great suffering and I know what the ship must be feeling with its makers gone, but I *don't* pretend to understand how you can send TR into intergalactic space!" Louahna replied. "I wouldn't have thought you'd do that."

[TR and Tab both insisted. It was their idea and Maita could do nothing to stop them. They tested a new theory of the drive and should be safe so long as they don't go to half the gravitational distance to the next galaxy. We're still understandably nervous. That isn't why we're here. We answer only to each other in such matters.]

"How could it be tested?" Heleemius asked.

"They went to New Zule to get some fastcoms after we gave what we had to the Searians," Z answered. "They jumped between the arm and the main part of the galaxy. Both Maita and TR can now use the mode between the spiral arms. They have it figured to the point it's no more dangerous than travel inside the galaxy."

TR seems to think it's solved a good part of the cross-drift problem. I hope it can find the ship and can return. The ship's been en route for more than six years so it'll take that long to return. Our problem is what's happening in the spiral arm, not what's happening out there.

"Six years would put it at more than halfway!" Louahna said.

[It only has a TTH one drive. We need more information about what's happening on the spiral arm. Why are you evading the question?]

"I can see it bothers you to discuss TR and Tab," Heleemius said, then rather sternly, "Please give them the information they seek, Louahna!"

They went aboard Maita and to room two where Maita projected everything they'd found on the holovid screen there. Louahna then gave the nav coordinates for all the planets she felt had been visited and/or interfered with. When they were all plotted they seemed to extend in a straight line from the tip of the arm inward along the outer edge with one planet in the main part of the galaxy.

"It goes in a line to near Ial and ends close to Elit and Exit on that end," Z mused, "Or does it go the other way?"

"The more recent contacts seem to be inward," Louahna replied.

[Great exploding galaxies! We're talking about a trip of more than twenty five thousand plazsis! Do they have TTH four or is this a longterm thing?]

"No," Z replied. "On what do you base the theory it started outward and moved in?"

"Nothing, really," Louahna answered. "It's only a feeling the people are.... It could be either way."

Have you met any on the inward side of the arm?

"I haven't had time to handle anything in there. Bursius has that area," Louahna replied.

[Please bring Bursius here. I see what Z means. This pattern tells us a great deal! I wish you had given us all this kind of information before. It would've saved us time. We've been in the wrong area.]

Louahna thought a bit, then disappeared. She returned three quarters of an hour later with Bursius, who said there was some indication some of his planets had been contacted a long time ago, but he simply made it another point of wonder for the populations so minimized the effects while preparing the people for contact in the far future.

"So we extend the line and project where it went next," Z suggested. "It's too bad Tab isn't here. We need to know a lot about his methods in tracing Searcher. This isn't a dangerous contact or even a protracted one. It's someone looking for something! *They're* searching for something specific."

[Our timing isn't so critical anymore. We'll have to find something dangerous and exciting or we'll go crazy with fear and worry about Tab and TR. This is another process thing that will eventually be valuable for us but, as I said, it isn't critical. We can simply follow along the line of travel and find them. A few days.]

"Let's go after Tab and TR!" Z suddenly said. "We can take a moder for the ship and can all come back here together!"

[I vote yes! It's dangerous and we'll share Tab and TR's fate! I vote yes!]

I refuse absolutely! – but I've been outvoted. Let's go to the nearest asteroid belt and gather the necessary minerals while Thing and I work out the math. We'll leave from the same point as TR and can find it through the sensors when we're close. I can detect use of TTH fourteen.

[Dumb! They won't be in TTH fourteen. They'll be in whatever substitutes for N space out there, but we can reach them fastcom within six thousand plazsis. Z will mine the raw minerals while you and I do our math bit. So long Louahna, Heleemius. Nice to meet you, Bursius. I'm sorry we had to call you from your work. We certainly wouldn't think of wasting your time.] (There was just the slightest emphasis on the "your".)

"I hope you won't think we're anxious to leave you," Z

explained. "We're anxious about TR and Tab. I know we should've heard from them by now. Tab will contact you if he returns and can't find us. Tell him to come after us if he's located the ship, but not to come if he hasn't.

"So long."

They left immediately and Maita located some asteroids with the necessary ores. Z gathered the ores and put them through the elementizer grid while Thing aided Maita with the math and they went to the same spot where TR made its first jump. They would try to follow TR exactly, but the drift factor would put them at some distance from TR's path each jump on an increasing scale. They should be able to come within fastcom range using side jumps in an expanding spiral pattern. They could detect the TTH1 drive from a greater distance than they could use the fast-com so that would prove easier to find with the wandering ship than to find Tab and TR.

They made a number of jumps, then stopped to use the longer range detectors, then halved the jumps when they felt they were far enough out to be close. Maita used the extra energy needed to keep the longrange detectors going constantly.

Maita could detect if TR used the TTH14 drive at any time, but got no indications.

Hmm. We seem to have jumped to one side or another too far to receive or send fastcom. I'll try jumping about randomly until we find something or something.

"Figure a flat plane between the two galaxies and jump from side to side on that plane," Z suggested. "I'm sure the ship'll stay very close to that plane in TTH one. TR might be following this same search method and we'll find the ship before it does, then we can wait for them to find us. Can't TR detect you in TTH fourteen out here?"

[You said something intelligent, Z! Amazing! That's twice in one year! You improve with age, I see.]

I can try to find an exact plane. Give me a minute. You two don't start. TR won't be looking in fourteen because it won't expect us to come out here. Yeah, right! TR knows us!

They waited until Maita jumped.

I find a very weak ... signal for the TTH one. I'll try to locate a direction.

They waited another few minutes, then Maita made a quick jump.

I have TR on fastcom now! They've turned and are en route back! I can ride a beam right to them. No I can't. They're too close. I'll jump ahead of them and run an intercept pattern in TTH one. We've found them! I can't believe it! We really found them! That's fantastic! I can't believe we've really managed to find them! The odds...! This is amazing! We did it! We actually found them! Umpty quadrillions of cubic plazsis out here and we actually found them!

[You mean you brought us clear out here and didn't believe you could actually find them? What the hell?! Are you out of your starjumping *mind*!?]

"Hooo, boy!" Z exclaimed.

Well, Z helped. I never would have found them that far off level plane. TR spent most of its time so far running a search pattern off the plane. Tab finally suggested the level-line approach. Tab's installing fastcom and we'll install the TTH fourteen moder. The ship only has a number that would be meaningless so we'll allow Z to come up with a fitting name.

"What was the name of its builders' race?" Z asked.

After a pause Maita said it was the Theronialtes from a

world they called Theronia.

"Okay! I hereby christen this ship the `Memoria de los Theronialtes,'" Z said. "We'll call you Theron for short."

[I like it.]

As do I.

"I do, too," TR said. "Theron agrees.

"What're you half-baked clowns doing out here in the middle of nowhaere? I thought you made another inviolable rule?"

*As soon as I say 'inviolable' I have to see if I was lying. Nobody can tell *me* what I can't do – even *me*!*

[We're going to emplace a moder for the TTH fourteen drive aboard our new friend, Theron, to facilitate its return to the Milky Way galaxy. Please cooperate in expediting that emplacement, all of you.]

"Emplace?" Tab asked. "Facilitate its return? Expedite the emplacement? Has Thing been eating thallium again?"

[At least *we* didn't waste umpty days running around in some ridiculous search pattern in an unlikely area looking for Theron!]

"You had nothing to do with that answer!" TR snapped. "Maita already gave you away when it sent me the stupid search pattern *you* followed, Rubber Puss!"

You were emplacing fastcom in a ship that wouldn't be in range for six years? I would have known better than that, you ambulatory gincha urn!

"Oh? You're going to *emplace* a TTH fourteen moder in a ship that wasn't designed to use it?" Tab shot back. "I know better than *that*!

"Have you considered for one second the mass/ volume ratio of Theron? Did you stop to figure this at all you platinum plated garbage scow?"

"What are you doing?!" Theron asked. "Am I to be reason

for you to fight among yourselves? It is better I go."

[You'll have to get used to this, Theron. We're very close and we often play this game. We came out here because we simply couldn't function properly while worrying so much about our best friends. This is a show of deep affec-tion. It just seems like an argument to those who don't know us, but it's really the way we show each other we care.]

"I understand," Theron replied. "There were many like that among my makers.

"What did Tab mean, my possible inability to control a TTH fourteen moder?"

*I'll interlink, start a timer cutoff and set the starting sequence before each jump. It'll take a short time after each jump for me to find you and to realign your controls, but we should be back inside the galaxy in two days maximum instead of six years. There's a race I want you to know and a machine who's a friend of ours. I'll feed you the sequence to prepare you for the TTH fourteen mode. It has strange effects on your sensors and will affect your reactions. You'll find it hard to control your anxiety, but I beg of you *don't* try to change the program in any way! You must be in a place where we can find you when we come back into N space.*

They spent fifty four hours doing the moder installation on Theron, becoming acquainted and learning all about its makers, who were much like the Maitans psychologically, but were very different physically. They made a short test jump that was reasonably within their predictions.

Three ship's days later they were back to the galactic rim and four days later grounded at the planoforming planet where Maita awakened Searcher to introduce it to Theron. Everybody exchanged information (And gossip) while Tab, Z and Thing installed the TTH4 on Theron. It couldn't be used in intergalactic space so TTH1 was left in place, but TTH14 was removed. Theron didn't want the mode. It didn't want to have to learn how to use it without Maita there to set the controls and argued that it was going to be of service to an organic society who had no real need of such fast travel. TTH4 was what the empire used on longer trips and TTH1 on shorter ones. Theron already had TTH1 so all that was necessary was adding some special-ized coils and the moder.

TR produced a multichannel fastcom unit with fixed stations directly to Searcher, Maita and TR. It also had all the empire standard channels the traders used along with the capacity to expand its frequencies tremendously. It also had a receiver for the new gravitics communications device TR was working on. If the control could be refined a bit it would have some advantages – that only the crew and close friends could use.

The emperor and its crew and the detective agency needed *one* little advantage now and then!

Theron would never again be alone.

When they were ready to go Tab went into Searcher to get some information with one of Maita's floaters.

I wanted to get some information from Searcher about its last project and the way it was programmed. Tab will stay with me to help decode the information. TRD Sixty will accompany Theron to New Zule where you will introduce those wonderful people to it and will find the best use to which to put Theron. I'm positive Theron will find peace and contentment with those people and a mutual love and respect will grow between you.

"I've been in contact with them," TR agreed. "They'll want to ask Theron to make regular delivery runs between University and Hospital where they're working on some project or other. They were going to ask Zeena to build them a ship, but this would be perfect! They know Zeena has orders for more ships than they could build in ten years and they need something much sooner.

"Zeena would be glad to stop work on everything else to make a ship for New Zule, but the Zulians would never permit any special treatment so they haven't mentioned anything to Zeena.

"Theron, you're gonna love those people! Maita and I go to New Zule just to be with them! I'll meet you guys when I have Theron settled."

Um-hmmm.

"Uh-oh!" TR cried.

You'll meet us when Theron's settled in so you can pick Tab up. Louahna has a little project for the Tabori R. DeSixtee Detective Agency.

[Oh, brother! Another Wahnee-type assignment? Can't we finish the one we're working on? This is totally uncon-scionable! Shee!]

We can handle what we were doing without Tab and TR now. We know what we're looking for and have a direction. It will be a simple matter of moving to a easily calculable interception point, not searching an enormous volume of space.

[I know! I want to be in on it and Tab gets to do so many of these things on his own. What's he doing in Searcher anyhow?]

"Oh-ho!" Z cried. "When does Tab learn about this?"

"I learned about it when you told TR," Tab said as he came in the port. "Thanks heaps!"

All right clowns! We're back and we need to get something positive done here for a change. We've wasted enough time getting nowhere. We have a lead so let's follow it.

"We seem to be following something like Searcher," Z said. "I just can't see what the object is. This one isn't looking to be found. It seems to be looking for something itself."

[While we still have Tab here we'd better trace the basic pattern. Maybe he can show us where to look. Put the whole thing in the holovid, Maita. All the stuff Louahna *should* have given us from the first.]

Now, Thing. Before you get down too hard on Louahna's inconsideration consider that we wouldn't have found Theron except for that, so the time definitely wasn't wasted.

[That was this one. We have to pin her right to the subject from now on if we do these things for her. She would have gone happily on her way if we got stuck out here for the next ten years!]

"She's irresponsible as all hell, but we have the necessary information now," Z said. "I agree. We have to pin her down in the future."

Maita showed the search pattern given to them by Louahna and Bursius and added what they'd found on their own.

"There doesn't seem to be a particular pattern. They moved along this arm and then will travel up the inside of the `Q' arm, then down and onto the `R' arm, then the `N' arm and so forth," Tab lectured. "My question would concern where they started. They seem to be going around the outer fringe of the galaxy. I suspect they're looking for something specific. We'll have to get closer to them to find the nature of their contacts. I can't picture what would be worth such a search! It would take several thousands of generations to entirely encircle the galaxy in that manner!

They aren't going very fast and are making a hell of a lot of stops.

"How about jumping straight across to the inner edge of the `Q' arm and trying to find a place they've been recently?"

I'm willing. They seem to have a slow drive. I'll say that much.

[I vote yes.]

"Let's go!" Z agreed.

They made the jump and Maita was pleased it had the TTH14 mode refined to where it was fairly predictable in intergalactic space.

Maybe we'll try a jump past the centerline between galaxies after we finish this job.

[Not with me aboard, you won't! You really have lost your star-hopping mind!]

Why not?

They spent a couple additional hours in deep mathematical discussions Z couldn't begin to understand so he went to the pilot's dome, ate a good meal, showered and took a nap.

Want to come to room two or should everyone come down there? was how he was awakened.

"The view's nice here," he answered.

A couple of minutes later the others came in and Thing climbed into Z's lap and rolled into a ball.

Thing never ceases to totally amaze me. It's figured intergalactic space. We can't go out of the sphere of influence of this galaxy unless we discover a new drive.

"Sure we can!" Z said. "Light does and radio does and, more importantly, you can detect TTH fourteen in other galaxies, so we can go there."

That started another mathematical argument so Z went back to sleep. Maita, Thing and Tab could argue silently.

Wake up, Z. We're ready to start our search.

Tab was gone, but Thing was still rolled into the ball in his lap.

[If it's of any importance to you, you may be right about being able to reach the next galaxy, but we have to use something other than TTH fourteen. The drift factor in fourteen condenses at the interpointal nexus and would make us tend to circle this galaxy in an odd moebus loop pattern along the confluences of the other galaxies a few thousand plazsis short of the midpoint lines of interstice nexi.]

"Go as close as you have good control, shift to TTH one until you reach the limit of drift there, which shouldn't be much, and shift to STL if you have to for a few light hours then reverse the process when you're in the influence sphere of the galaxy you want to visit."

Give us the math.

"You know perfectly well I ain't got no damn math!" Z said. "Light and other things travel between the galaxies so we can, too. Don't start another stupid argument now. I don't want or need anymore sleep!

"What's the plan? Just bumble around like we usually do?"

Tab came from the elevator. "There are certain obvious places to look," he said. "If we find nothing we move inward. They aren't here yet."

I'll have to figure points to drop off relays. We aren't in touch with the empire at the moment and that's illegal. I break my own laws when I go intergalactic. We may as well put in more relays while we're here. It'll save a trip later and it's nice to know we can scream for help if we have to.

[Let's place the relays first so TR can find us when it comes back. We may need other calls, but TR will *have* to make them if it's to find us to pick up Tab.]

"We can wait a year or so!" Tab said. "TR can handle a case or two on its own!"

"Too late!" Z returned. "You've already been tagged for this one!"

It took them six hours to deploy relays down the center of the arm, but the system now put everywhere on the spiral arm into the fastcom chain of the empire. Traders could now come out if they found any reason to come – and they definitely would!

They then went back to the point where they would start their search.

They found a planet that had been visited the third one they tried.

The people were hard to classify, having both reptilian and mammalian traits. They were fairly primitive, but the floaters found there had been "Strange beings from the sky" in the time of the probe subject's grandparents. The planet was called Inny by the natives, so was registered as that.

The next two planets that had been visited were found in star systems quite close (relatively) to each other and were both peopled by reptilian intelligences. They were entering an early industrial age in the first, Neekhth, and were in a tribal stage on the other, Sorn. Next was a planet called Bleech by its inhabitants. It was peopled by a mammalian society who lived on a nearly perfect planet and had life much too easy so they were extremely lazy. A number of the people remembered seeing space visitors, but were unaffected by contact so Maita landed for the crew to question some of the citizens.

TRD-60 came to get Tab and to head back to Neeahna for the meeting with Louahna, leaving just Maita, Thing and Z to carry on with the search.

Theron was immensely happy and delighted with the Zulians and had formed a strong and close friendship with Searcher and TR. It would make four scheduled runs yearly to University, various runs to Hospital while the research was underway and exploratory trips at all other times.

"Have you figured a way to name individual Zulians?" Z asked of TR.

"Yes. We do it digitally," TR replied. "It's not important to them. I rather imagine Theron will learn their names and will develop special friendships. That will be the more natural thing."

[We can feel good about that.]

There was no disagreement about that point!

Thing and Z were sitting on a bench at the beach talking with two of the Bleech who had seen the alien ship. One was a female called Rohn, the other a male called Fahr.

[We want some information about those people and their ship. They're causing problems among some peoples and may not be aware of it. From what we've found to this point we don't believe they want to cause any harm to anyone.]

"Well," Rohn replied, "they had an enormous globular ship that stayed high, while six – I think it was six, wasn't it Fahr? – came on a smaller ship. About half the size of the one that came to take your friend away."

"Yes. There were six," Fahr said. "At least six left the ship. There may have been any number more who stayed inside."

[Were they armed?]

"What do you mean?" Rohn asked.

"Were they carrying weapons?" Z asked.

"Weapons?" Fahr asked. "That's one of the ancient words. We wouldn't know a weapon if we saw one. What does one look like?

"They had a lot of machines dangling from belts and carrier bags on their, I guess you'd say shoulders."

[What did the people look like?]

"They were strange looking," Rohn said. "Not as strange as you, but very different."

"Oh, yes," Fahr added. "All those extra arms and the feeler things on their heads and those strange eyes – I guess they were eyes. Lots of little hexagons in big bulges across the tops of their heads."

"Oh, my god!" Z exclaimed. "Did they have chitin? I mean, were they covered in material like the top of this table?"

"Yes!" Rohn cried. "Sort of orangey! Like clawfish!"

[We're being asked to return to our ship. I'm sorry to have to leave such pleasant company, but we're on duty. Thank you so much for your kind hospitality.]

Z looked puzzled as he helped Thing onto its floater. They quickly went to Maita.

"What's the problem, Maita?" Z asked as soon as they were aboard.

[You don't know?]

"Not really. What's going on?"

You've pretty well established that these things are insects!

"So? They're insects," Z said. "That's no reason to get so excited."

What!?

[Wait, Maita. He's right. They haven't done one single thing to deliberately harm anyone. In fact they seem to be going to extremes to *avoid* hurting anyone! We must remain rational.]

I have trouble with that. I have very strong memories of the Pweetoos.

"I have even stronger memories of the Immins and they were mammals," Z replied. "We have no reason to suspect these people of anything except perhaps a little bit of ignorance. They may have no conception of what kinds of damage they may cause. It could also be far beyond their ability to understand."

[Z's right. We must remain rational. They might even be a very good race. Of all of us, *you* should know that exteriors are meaningless.]

"They're looking for something very specific. They stay on a particular planet for only a day or two, then leave," Z mused. "They're staying right on the rim for some reason.

"We have to meet them to find what they're after. I admit I don't have a clue! This is a project that will take millennia so I suppose insects would be the ones who would do it."

[I believe we'll meet them very soon now. They were here only seven years ago and have a very slow drive we don't even know so we're very close to them.]

"Let's find them. I'm curious," Z said. "I don't think these people are going to be anything like the Pweetoos and I'll soon go nutzier than I already am if I don't find out what they're after!"

They soon left Bleech and stopped at one system that had only barren planets, then found another, Chamrey, with a culture that was fairly well advanced into an iron age. The people were rather strange and unclassifiable.

The floaters returned to report and Maita said, *They left here less than a year ago.*

"We don't have much evidence they use even radio," Z said. "I don't know if that's because they don't have it or what."

[Maita? Can you figure when they were here to the minute from what you've learned?]

To the hour, yes. Why?

[Go to where the radio they used when they were here will be. See if they *did* use any. It may be a thing they only use ship to ship.]

"Good idea! We'd have the right wavelengths and all," Z said. "That way we could call them from anywhere in a system when we get close."

They jumped out past the likely position and waited. Four and a half hours later Maita announced they used radio between the ship and the landing craft.

This is a language not unlike the Pweetoos and Klatch. It will necessitate a translator for you, Z.

"We can find them if we monitor those wavelengths. Send a signal...." Z said. "No. We'll have to be pretty close. You should be able to figure where they should be by now from the length of their trip and the time it took between Bleech and Chamrey. We can look in that area."

Maita quickly figured the likely area where the ship would be and jumped. They made a short search until Z suddenly cried, "Holy shit!"

There was a globular ship in the scanner that was easily two kilometers in diameter.

I'm getting an answer on their radio, but I can't begin to understand any of it.

[We have to get one of them on the headgear. We're not

in a position to know context for learning the language otherwise. There's no other way.]

It might not work on them.

"Use the system you learned from that place that sent the instructions," Z suggested, referring to a world they found many years ago that had an efficient system based on obvious symbols. It drew pictures through radio.

[That was a sort of primitive television trick. Do they have it, Maita?]

I'll draw a radio dot picture. If they receive a printed copy it'll show. It'll take awhile.

Three hours later Maita reported it had a list of some words. The Freenz had some black and white television of low resolution. They would expect Z to come aboard.

Z took the list and a floater with the translator and a space-shielded atmosphere across to where there was a bright flashing light. There was a headgear on the floater the Freenz had agreed to try. Z suggested it had worked on the Klatch and Pweetoos so it would probably work as well on the Freenz.

He was led into a warm, strange-smelling area that opened into a vast hydroponic garden where he was met by a strange obviously insectoid being. It was in three segments. The lower was carried behind and low and was a roundish cylinder with a sharp "waist" between it and the center section. There were two legs near the waist. The center section had two sets of arms, the lower pair of which could substitute for extra legs. There was another thin section that worked as a neck with a triangular head with large compound eyes, four short antennae, mandibles and whiskers that hung like a beard. Breathing was handled by openings along the lower and center sections.

The Freenz rolled its head from side to side, which Z took

to be a greeting, so he held his hands out palms up and nodded.

The Freenz then waved for him to follow it so he trotted along behind it for what he estimated to be a kilometer. They came to a large hole that extended out of sight both upward and downward. The Freenz stepped into the open hole and rose quickly upward. It pointed to a yellow spot as it entered so Z stepped into the hole at the same spot.

That took some nerve! It was like stepping into a bottomless pit!

He felt the gravitic grappler touch him and he rose about five meters below the guide. The guide pointed to a green line along the partial wall, then leaned toward it. Z did the same and found himself standing just outside another floor. He had risen at least four hundred meters.

The guide waited for him, then led the way along a hallway.

They were now in an area of many branching side tunnels. The guide pointed to a chartreuse and yellow line which they stayed on until they came to a large door, which they entered.

There were approximately fifty of the Freenz in the room. He stood while they studied him carefully, then one came to make a short speech. The floater translator was able to translate part of it. It was a diplomatic greeting that said basically that the Freenz were glad to finally meet a race that had developed as far as they if not much further and they sincerely hoped their race would be able to trade some much-needed information.

Z answered that he spoke for the Maitan Empire in greeting their brothers in space.

He thought he'd made a blunder, but the translator was being controlled by Maita so covered the gaff of saying "brothers" to what were almost certainly females.

It was obvious the translator wasn't doing a very good job. Z held up the headgear and said, "This will give us your language. It will read everything in the mind of the subject if it works as we hope.

"Will anyone volunteer to use the machine?"

One of the Freenz stepped forward to announce something about being a language teacher, then bowed its head for Z to place the helmet.

The reading took almost an hour, during which the Freenz sat patiently. When it was complete Z offered his sympathy to the Freenz who had used the probe machine, explaining he had used the machine and knew the severe type of headache it caused and this was an unusually difficult reading.

Just say it. Z. I have the language. It worked.

"I wish to apologize for the side-effects of the machine. I've used it myself and know it's far from pleasant," he said. "If you will go to a dark place where it's quiet the worst effects will pass fairly quickly."

"Thank you," the Freenz replied. "The pain is intense so I will eat some strong drugs and, therefore, will be of no use for several srrzurs.

"I am pleased the machine worked well."

It turned, nodded at the others, then left.

"I am called Lok and am the scientific adviser to this ship," another Freenz said. "I am certain we have much information to exchange and may be of some aid one to the other.

"We are a curious race, which is why we find ourselves in this most difficult situation."

"We've noted you've met many races in the past," Z said. "We feel you're searching for something. I'm aware you're not familiar enough with mammals' forms of psychology or reptilian psychology to realize those contacts can be very dangerous to the development of some races.

"May we ask what you seek?"

"I am called Plo," another answered. "I am our ship historian. This is head administrator Ziss and the teacher is called Meem.

"We have tried to be aground on a planet only in very small numbers and for very limited timespans. There is information we must seek, but we have great trouble communicating. The last world but one seemed to be welcoming us to stay, but we could not be sure."

"The Bleech?" Z asked. "They would welcome you, yes. You would do no damage to them and would become close friends with little trouble. They are a friendly and curious race."

"You asked what we seek," Plo continued. "I will tell you.

"There was once a ship that was built by a race, the Freenz. It was to be a wonderful experiment where we would go to space to meet other strange and wonderful people on many different worlds. The ship would be a self-contained world in itself. We knew it would take many years to reach those other worlds.

"The drive was untested in such a ship, though the theory was sound and small tests with models performed exactly as predicted to the theory.

"The ship was built in orbit, stocked and eventually a colony was ready to be launched in our quest for companionship along the trail of life in the universe!

"Something went terribly wrong. We suddenly found ourselves far from the galaxy – so far it took more than four years to get back within its confines. We did not know where we were. We could not even be certain we were in the same galaxy. All we knew was that our home is on the rim of a spiral arm. Nothing was familiar. We have now been searching now for nine hundred twenty one years and three drznths.

"I am sure that, as the ship was lost with three thousand of the Freenz aboard, they would never attempt such a dangerous thing again. What we seek is home. It is that simple.

"You seem to travel very quickly. We can but hope you will be able to save us many more sad centuries of searching. Perhaps studying our vessel and the very complete and careful records we keep will prove of great value to you. Perhaps you will be able to find what happened to our ship to make it go so very far so very quickly."

"I'm sure we can," Z replied. "We have a very large empire and can start a search with many thousands of ships. We should find your home world soon."

Z, I think I know what happened here. This will be in both Maitan and Freenz so all can understand. The builders of the ship didn't have the math yet to tell them the mass of the ship would interfere with the moders. It's designed to travel in TTH one, but was shifted to another plane much as TRD Sixty, an empire ship, once did while trying to jump from the surface of a planet. That much mass affects the moder, shifting the phases and plunging your ship into TTH fourteen where the cross-drift factor threw you outside of the galaxy. The moder formed a harmonic and phased out altogether very quickly, but you were far from where you started. I have sent a call for information and need to know some things, Lok. Do your people use radio on the bands you use in the ship?

"Yes. I am certain they will monitor the channel forever

or until we return," Lok replied. "It is held in frequency with a carbon crystal of very precise size and shape and purity. It does not vary."

Very well. I'll transmit the features of your language and will deploy ships to listen and to transmit the message in your language and on that frequency, `We are well and are coming home.' Does that meet with your approval?

"We can never hope to repay you," Plo said. "We have been many generations here and are very tired and very frustrated. If you find our home for us we will do all work for you for five thousand generations."

"You'll owe us nothing," Z replied. "It's a service that's done for any and all by the empire. If you wish you may send a delegation or go yourselves to Maita to await an answer to our inquiries."

"Ziss and Lok will go with you," Plo replied. "As head administrator I am forbidden to leave the ship.

"I know we have very little hope of surviving to see Freenz ourselves, but just the knowledge we are going to return in our progeny is enough to give us great joy."

Perhaps we'll discover a way to get all of you home in a relatively short time. I'll expect Lok and Ziss aboard momentarily. I'm sure Z will wish to study your ship for awhile. He's very greatly impressed by what you've accomplished, as am I.

"It's truly amazing, Maita!" Z said. "This ship is a whole self-contained world! They're growing food and living much as farmers do in any culture. It's really fantastic!

"I'll appreciate a short tour before I return to Maita."

The Freenz were quite pleased that Z could appreciate the way the ship was made and run. They showed him the drive engines, which meant nothing to him, though the floater scanned everything.

The food was grown on several levels and the purified air was circulated through the crops. The light was carefully controlled, as was temperature. The moisture actually rose to the next floor upward where fans were turned on at specific times through vane coolers causing it to quite literally rain on the crops below. Some of the water was taken from special vanes for drinking and other uses. It was pure distilled water.

There were bunks in long rows in a special section. The Freenz required no privacy. The food preparation area was clean and efficient, waste disposal went directly to composting with plant material. The generators were of several types and were clean and perfectly maintained – which was logical. Insectoids were bred for those specific jobs. They did those jobs. Perfectly.

Z wondered if he should ask about that, decided "What the hell!" – and did.

"Yes," Lok answered. "That was very hard for us to understand about others at first, that they must be trained for a job and even did jobs they were not suited for. It was a very strange thing for us, but we have seen in our travels that we are the strange ones. We have not found another society much like ours so have reached the conclusion such societies are very rare.

"My personal theory is that we are very slow in developing these things – much slower than mammals or reptiles or others, but we are more sure. There are many things lost in many places we have seen, but we do not lose anything. Ever.

"Perhaps we would not make the same mistake so many times because we would learn very quickly those things that do not work. That is why we know there will have been no other ships of this kind. We were lost, so the ship did not work, so it won't be repeated. Also, this ship took large parts of our resources.

"Friend Z! If you can get our progeny home the Freenz will never forget that, either! Never!"

"Friend Lok, I intend to get *you* home!" Z replied.

Chapter three

The Freenz prepared a small ship and Z and Meem joined Lok and Plo in it. The Freenz were afraid Maita would be unable to take them aboard without them suiting up, a long and difficult process for them.

Maita spun a rubbery tubular chamber that attached around the airlock on their vessel and around its own cargo door. There was no problem and only a few minutes' delay. Maita sent a small recording floater to the Freenz ship to inspect the engines and drive to see what it would entail to modify them to increase the ship's relspeed. The scan from Z's tour wasn't complete enough, but had shown it wouldn't be an insurmountable task. The coils and drive units were exceptionally well constructed and were in perfectly maintained condition. There should be little necessary to get them in phase again.

The Freenz were amazed and delighted by the things they saw in Maita and were very curious about Thing. They had visited three hundred seven planets with highly evolved ecosystems in the past nine hundred years and had never seen anything like it. Meem said they never found anything like themselves either, so were glad to know they were in such good company in being unique!

Thing explained that the empire had found only two advanced insectoid races before, the Freenz making the third. It got into a discussion about how the Freenz were so much less specialized and structured than others they had found. At first Plo didn't understand what Thing meant.

"The other two cultures worked on the fixed principle that an individual was bred and raised for a single specific job and couldn't do anything else," Z explained. "You people seem to be able to handle a number of different jobs. I discussed it with Lok aboard your ship."

"Oh!" Plo said. "I understand. We have met many mammalian societies and as many or more reptilian ones. We have made note of the variety of functions each member appears to be able to handle.

"Some of us are bred to perform abstract mental or varied physical tasks, though most members of the colony are single function.

"The farmers are only that. Farmers. They can not be anything other.

"The military, which we are fortunate to need few of, thank the Great Guidance, serve no other function.

"Lok is bred to have more ability in scientific pursuits than others, but we haven't the gene pool to get what we so greatly need – a true abstract thinker. The race *can* produce them, rather obviously, or we wouldn't have the ship.

"Of course, we wouldn't be in this situation either. There are positive and negative aspects to most things we have found. The value of random intelligence such as yours is that you can see very quickly how to solve a problem, but we must spend many generations at it. The lack of highly developed insectoid races is undoubtably due to the very slow increase of variables in our races.

"As a historian I realize also that we were most fortunate we were not of the warlike members of our types or we would have been lost in far history to interclan rivalries. Our racial evolution would have ground to a halt."

[You're the most advanced of the insectoid races we've met. One no longer exists due very directly to its inability to overcome certain structured reactions. They could tolerate none of their own kind within a certain limited territory.]

"Yes," Plo replied. "The Freenz, too, were once very territorial, but we evolved past that. It isn't a thing I could believe would serve any race well beyond the time when there is competition for food, thus before mass farming procedures are developed. It is strange these you speak of ever knew space travel."

"To tell the truth we tended to be suspicious of you when we first met," Z said. "This ship's makers, the original world of Maitans, were totally destroyed except for a very small number who escaped on a single ship and one small colony lost on another world thousands of years before.

"They were destroyed by the Pweetoos, an insectoid race.

"The Pweetoos were the ones who were so overly territorial – and you're right. They didn't find space travel. The Maitans gave it to them. The other race, the Klatch, were a race we could never hope to understand. Their reactions toward us, as we saw them, were as much as insane. I am sure they found us as insane. There is no point of understanding between out societies."

"I understand this," Lok said. "I have studied the psychologies of many kinds of races and, while I make no apologies for any race other than my own, which needs make no apologies, I understand why insectoid societies would present great problems to other races. They also would present problems to one another, no doubt.

"You have stated you realize that you seem insane to those who seem insane to you."

*Not really. The Klatch were in small groups, each with its own queen. They felt we were there to invade them and fought until we were able to make the queens see we would leave if we were given the information we sought. They were merely highly territorial. The Pweetoos would war on one another if there was more than one queen on a planet.

They used trickery to destroy the Maitans and had no moral sense whatever. They destroyed forty one civilizations using dephased moders to explode the suns of the systems. If you understand anything about the moders in your ship you know they destroyed the planets and suns in the other plane the moders dephased in.*

"They had instincts and no real intelligence if they would do such a thing!" Plo cried. "It is no wonder such a race did not find space travel for themselves!"

[The Maitans took them in as friends and were overthrown when they allowed the Pweetoos to breed the pilots for their ships. The Maitans trusted too much. That's why we worry so much when undeveloped civilizations are contacted.]

"You then led a revolt against these Pweetoos, Maita?" Plo asked.

Yes. We had to destroy the broods on several planets to stop them. When the queen died the brood died out.

"It is probably best they were destroyed," Lok said. "If they decided to expand their worlds they would have destroyed any world that resisted them. I do not think any race could discover space travel on its own and be such a society. They would destroy themselves first with the basic technology."

"I fully agree," Z replied. "We've had as much trouble with a mammalian society – race. The Immins. They were contacted by the Maitans before they were ready and became a horrible problem to everyone of any race who met them. We wiped out most of them and have restricted the remainder to the planet Orta.

"It isn't only insectoid cultures who do these things."

Thank you, Z. I remember how you reacted to Sisstuh and Fesch the first time you met them and I know my reactions have been as poorly considered as were your own. The Kheth soon became your close friends as I'm sure these people will become mine. There are more than two thousand ships scanning all the galactic arms and fringe spaces for your home and my floater has returned. I'll serve a good meal that's suited to your systems and you may use room nine to relax and wait while we seek. Thing will please assist me in seeing how we may modify either your drive or your ship to where it'll take you home in less than a year.

Z showed them where room nine was and suggested they instruct the servo about building them a comfortable spot to rest, then went to the pilot's dome where Thing curled up in his lap to help decipher the drive of the Freenz ship.

I would have wagered we would never meet an insect society that had a place in the empire and I'm still not certain. I tend to think these will be no problem to anyone, but don't like the idea of individuals being bred for a specific purpose. It's no better than slavery.

[Nonsense, Maita! It's their way! You have no trouble using servos. The workers are nothing more – nor less – than organic servos. Z can tell you if he saw any signs of mistreatment while he was on that ship?]

"No," Z replied. "They seemed content to be doing what they were doing. The only ones who seemed in any way unhappy were the elite such as these here. They were frustrated and feared the quest, as they call it, was hopeless. They only kept going on because they were bred to lead, so they must lead.

"I believe they actually care for the farmers and soldiers and feel a terrible responsibility for them. They only do what they were bred to do and are content at that, just as Maita was built and programmed to be a spaceship and is happiest when it's being a spaceship.

"I *am* amazed at one thing, though! Look how far I've come! I went to them expecting to be treated as a friend, not full of suspicion – and I was treated very well!

"I think I'm finally growing up."

*Now it's up to me to mature. I'm afraid and suspicious, and I have no real reason to be. These people have done no wrong nor harm to anyone. They seem to make no judgments and are highly intelligent, even if that intelligence *is* highly directed. Your point about the Immins is well-taken. I *will* be objective about these people. I'll probably learn to like them.*

[You're over the worst, Maita. You called them people and not things. I get only slight empathic feeling from them, but they're a caring and sympathetic people even if it is almost all directed toward their own kind. Time will tell, but they do know they stand no chance against us. I don't think they have any feelings except they want to go home. They're very tired with a tiredness that comes from generations of doing a duty that has lost all meaning. We give them hope. These elite, as Z calls them, keep going to care for the others and for no other reason. I think they're good people. Their drive is much like TTH one and is exceptionally well-constructed. Our problem is too much mass. Far too much of it. We can handle that I think.]

Maita and Thing started discussing the Freenz ship while Z dozed. When Z awoke Thing was gone and the dome was darkened.

"Maita?"

Yes, Z?

"Have you figured a way to move that ship faster?"

Yes. Several possibilities occurred to us. It'll depend on what the Freenz want to do and what they can do without.

"Are they still in nine?"

No. Thing's having a great time discussing history with Plo in room two. Come on up! It's truly fascinating! Plo remembers through a mnemonic system it's bred for. She. They're all females here. The written history is constantly updated by Plo when anything happens. I'm gathering very good information about hundreds of planets they've visited. It's fascinating! I'm learning from them! They've told us of several places we must see. Come on up!

Z grinned and went to room two where Thing was sitting in the center of a circle of three huge insects and listening as Plo told of a planet that was visited three generations past.

"... rocky with many plants of great variety. Most of the plants had evolved defenses such as sharp thorns and poisonous excretions while the animals had evolved defenses of their own. The dominant race is amphibious and reptilian. They are large and ferocious carnivores and cannot possibly advance much more because they fight constantly.

"The Bleech, as you call them, are the contrast that proves the theory, though these things are extremely variable. An easy planet will often produce a race that is lazy and hedonistic, but who will probably not advance beyond a certain point. There is no reason to advance as there is no challenge to the life force. The life force, like electricity, must have a resistance applied to become useful.

"These others, those on very hard planets, are usually overly aggressive so eventually destroy themselves. Also like electricity, if too much resistance is applied the current stops. The range between extremes is where we are able to best use electricity and where the life force best advances a race.

"The next planet was a mostly water world and is at coordinate two hundred seventeen. It is a pleasant place for those who like the humidity and water but, as insectoids of a drier evolution we don't care much for those worlds. There are only semi-intelligent beings there. They fit the pattern of the too-easy planet.

"Next we found a planet, coordinate two hundred eighteen, that was very strange in that it held more than forty percent iron in its crust. There were nickel and those related elements in large concentrations as well. Those elements are always found together it seems.

"The air was very difficult for Treeb so the team did not disembark from the survey ship. There were strange beings there with iron shells filled with catalytic reagents. They ate the rocks directly and would internally refine it in the same manner as do some bacteria. We had many navigational problems there as the world was a huge, very strong magnet. The fields interfered with sensitive equipment for a half year.

"Next, at coordinate two hundred nineteen, we found a very high-pressure planet. Treeb died there and Lurb took over the historian duties. The dominant lifeform there is a single-celled being. It is almost a meter across and joins with several others to form a single new `bud' that develops into a new being. It seems there are six varied sexes and two neutrals. The genes are far more complex than anything we have ever before seen. We did not know they were intelligent and actually killed one. The scientific coordinator then, Annine, soon discovered `mind' material and was horrified. The discovery we had done this was traumatic to our race and caused a crisis.

"A great advantage of our race is that we have the administrator who accepts full responsibility and blame for all things. Bleeve offered her life to the people, but they were able to communicate that we could not know. They had no idea that *we* were intelligent until we accepted responsibility for the act and we left with a far better understanding of one another. We are much alike in spirit while very different of aspect. We could be friends with such as these who can understand people who are so very alien as we.

"At two hundred twenty there is a system with three planets where each has advanced lifeforms. They are all on moderately easy planets and are not very aggressive – except those on the outermost of the inhabited worlds. We generally do not do anything to influence other races, but we did so there. It was a difficult decision and we have no real imperative in these matters, but we *do* have consciences and we do feel that any being must aid any other in certain rare situations that may arise.

"The full guiding council and the precedents in our history finally decided us. We must act or we will never again know inner peace. Our duty is to all, not only to Freenz. We cannot become part of a larger entity should we consider only ourselves. That is a limit one imposes on itself or throws from itself.

"We remained on that world for twelve days and impressed in their minds that we would return every few decades without warning. If they took their militarism to any other planet we would crush them without mercy. We are thousands of years advanced over them and will tolerate no spread of that foolishness. We made the point plainly that they must either solve their aggressiveness or never leave their own world.

"That system is a place where differing cultures will meet before going through the cleansing process of finding methods of interstellar travel. We will argue this was a case where we did the greatest good for all by premature contact. My conscience tells me we must find a way to go back as we warned them we will to ensure they do not harm their neighbors. It was our word."

I agree fully. I've prepared a meal I hope you will enjoy tremendously. I'll have a servo bring it in. We can then continue this fascinating account when we've finished dining.

They had a large meal as delicious as Maita promised. They thanked them and explained that food variety was necessarily very limited on their ship. They were basically herbivorous and grew the plants that had proven most valuable in producing nutritious food with a small sacrificing of some taste, though what they used now was somewhat better than what their ancestors subsisted on.

After the meal they talked about some of the worlds Maita had visited and told stories of the empire, the pirates, the insane machine (*You see? It's not only *organic* societies who screw up! *any*one can!*) and even the Pweetoo wars. The Freenz were deeply interested in the whole narrative and then talked of much of the time they spent in space personally. Plo told them of the quest to the present moment, starting from when she broke off for the meal. She knew all the details of each world they visited and was a good storyteller, well able to hold her audience.

As the Freenz ship had no exterior view ports or domes they were excited when invited to visit the O dome to watch the stars for a short while. None of the present group of leaders had seen the outside of their ship except for the survey leader. It was too difficult a process for them to suit up to go outside.

They talked about the magnificent ship a few minutes and

were preparing to leave the dome when an indistinct outline stepped through the wall.

"This is Louahna," she announced. "Maita will translate on the floater for me so the Freenz will understand. Maita called me here to meet these rare people and Heleemius will be here soon. I'm fascinated at the things they've endured and the things they've accomplished.

"Ah, here's Heleemius now – and Zianteus."

Two more fuzzy outlines stepped through the floor.

"How interesting!" Lok cried. "What manner of strange beings are these? This is fascinating!"

Maita introduced the M82nds and explained their dual-planal existence.

"Maita has requested that we try to locate your home world," Zianteus explained. "It will be some while before everyone is contacted, but we'll try. There's a slight chance one of us has been to your home planet."

They all went to room two – Z, Thing, Lok, Plo and Meem took the elevator. The M82nds stepped through the floor. They chatted awhile until Maita announced they may soon have a definite word.

We believe our friend, Rollo, the Acnian Fleet captain, has detected the radio impulses from the general area and merely has to follow them in to the world. He has to move quite slowly as he doesn't have the sensitive triangulation equipment I do.

The Freenz were trying hard to contain their growing excitement, but weren't having complete success.

[Please don't get too highly elated about this yet. It could be a false alarm. It may be nothing. It could be another race who happen to use the same frequency or even a natural phenomenon.]

"We will try," Lok said. "You must realize! It has been so

very long! We didn't truly expect any chance we would see our home!"

A fuzzy outline stepped through the wall, spoke with Louahna and Heleemius for a short while, then stepped away again.

"That was Plotius," Heleemius explained. "He couldn't stay. He's been busy working with four separate cultures and is having some trouble.

"The Freenz world is located at E three twelve and oh, N seventeen nine ninety seven. It's good we've found the world, but it's almost directly across the galaxy from here.

"We're happy for you, our new friends. You can go home now. We're happy to know a new kind of people. We wish you well."

The Freenz were so excited they were trembling all over.

Rollo just sent a com message that Freenz is located almost precisely where Plotius estimated the coordinates to be. He told your home world you're well and will soon be returning. He says they're already planning a huge celebration in your honor.

[We'll have to modify your ship. Have you designed in a way whereunder you can jettison a large portion of it? We've got to reduce the mass by a very large factor. It's simply impractical to chance moving that huge amount of material through the more complex planal interfaces.]

"We can quickly dismantle much of it," Plo replied. "We have not dared. We knew not how long we would need it. We can remove enough that we can return home with the needed supplies, but we must know exactly how long that will be to plan the voyage properly."

[It's forty one thousand five hundred thirteen plazsis in TTH one. That's ... six thousand nine hundred hours or nearly one empire year. How many of you are now on the ship? I need exact figures.]

"We have two hundred larvae and one thousand adults," Lok said. "We will hatch no more so the larvae will emerge at the rate of two per day while the adults will die at about the same rate."

[Mmm. That'll be roughly thirty thousand metric tons of food, assuming a ten percent delay. We'll take some extra. How much is ready now?]

"We have about twelve tons at a given time, but the harvest of all the gardens will make that with many tons extra," Lok said.

The drive engines can be carried to the top section of the ship. They'll be far more efficient there. Using the four top floors will give us the needed mass reduction and should leave ample space for your people to be comfor-table. How long will it take to detach the rest of the ship? There's no longer any rush. You'll be home in a year instead of the eleven hundred it would have taken on your present course and pattern. You must be most careful – I need not remind you – that you don't lose your air and that nothing else can leak. You won't be able to grow anything or to renew air, though I'll put in an elementizer to ensure oxygen and water. I need a rough estimate of the time before you're ready.

"We can do it in little time. The levels are sealed except for the center carrier shaft and that is only twenty two meters across," Plo replied, "Moving the drive engines is the hardest part and will take the longest time. They are bulky and sensitive. We must be careful there or we could do damage that would be very slow to repair."

[When can you have the harvest completed? Including moving, drying, whatever is necessary to preserve it all for your use on the trip.]

"In two days," Lok estimated. "We can have the ship separated in that time. I estimate it will take six days to move the motors."

I'll move the entire drive with my servos and ask that you harvest nothing. I'll also ask that you remove all but the top two sections. It will make it close, but not uncomfortable. I'll have the drive moved.... Be ready to leave in two days!

[What's your plan, Maita? They'll need their food. You'll need the bulk elements even with the synthetic food machines – and we're talking about thousands of people. Do you intend to modify the drive? You could ... oh! Yes! It would work!]

I'm building a TTH four moder right now to fit that drive. Removal of that mass means it WILL work! You are expected home on Freenz in eighty seven days! We have to hurry! We certainly don't want to be so gauche as to keep the celebration waiting! That wouldn't be fair to your people!

The Freenz were staring in disbelief.

"Awright! Less gawking and more action!" Z ordered. "Standing here isn't going to get those bulkheads split! Food for eighty seven days! Move everything that needs moving! Compress your air in the lower sections and store it for emergency use! Water must be carried and stored! The larvae must be attended to! Let's get moving here, people! Hup! Hup!"

[Pay no attention to Z. He tends to get carried away – and to start giving orders. We just ignore him. You'll wish to get all of this ready for the trip so we'll have you return to give the good news to your people.]

Tell them they're going home!

The Freenz were totally efficient in moving the foodstuffs

and the equipment that would prove necessary into the "top" of the spherical ship. The flight controls and bridge were already up there in a sort of domed structure so some time was saved there. They'd built the ship with dual plating between levels so Maita had them seal both openings as they separated them.

Heleemius, who had dropped in again, would arrange for the Zeenans to install a preset TTH1 mode drive that would cause the bottom portion of the ship to deliver itself to Freenz in about two years. The automatics would keep everything on board in good order.

[It would be a terrible shame for the race to lose the tremendous resources spent on the ship, which can be orbited around Freenz and used as a research station and hospital.]

I agree. How long did it take to build the ship, Plo?

Plo, who was with Lok in room two of Maita, was helping the coordination of efforts and was using Maita's communications to keep in contact with Ziss and the "foremen" inside the Freenz ship.

"The project was begun just twenty two years Freenz before it was ready to launch on the quest," Plo said. "That would be perhaps thirty three years Maitan if my estimations are correct. The planet has used a large part of its natural materials constructing the project and will very certainly welcome its return. Those things are needed, I am sure. We must find a way to someday repay the Maitan Empire and especially you and your crew for their aid and kindnesses. We owe a debt to the M Eighty Seconds that is beyond price, too."

"That's what we're here for," Z said. "It gives us something useful to do. I'm sure the traders guild will make arrangements to get your people all the raw materials they could want of any type at all. Your people are perfectly adapted to producing the most delicate and exacting work so you'll soon find yourselves in great demand in the production of such things as positronic equipment and that kind of stuff. The demand is huge and grows every time a new world enters the empire or something new is invented.

"I'd think such things as the drive coils – you could make a deal with Zeena! They produce the best ships in the galaxy and they're always looking for someone to produce the focusing units for the engines. If they're done as well as those in your ship you've got that market tied tight.

"Rollo says they're already making progress in setting up a deal to produce the sensory links for the major moder producers on Ternz. That's the only comparative weakness in TCs. The TC moder wasn't as stable as the Zeenan ones. Now Ternz can compete on an equal basis."

"I do not understand this!" Lok said. "It was only slightly more than one day past when your friend, Rollo, first contacted Freenz! How could these traders on this Ternz even know of the existence of Freenz in so short a time and how could they have possibly worked out an ability to communicate? How can Rollo communicate?

"It is beyond my ability to understand!"

[Simple. Heleemius took a language crystal to Rollo and the Acnians placed a fastcom relay satellite on grid that includes an automatic translator device. Rollo put the translator into the empire network so now the languages of any member or associate of the Maitan Empire can be automatically translated into Freenz and vice versa. The entire system's open to you now. By the time you get home there will be hundreds of trade routes that include Freenz. The traders will know you're going to be able to produce quality goods so every last one of them will try to get a contract for something!]

Yes. I have a message I wish to give to the entire quest ship before you begin your journey home. It's to be a surprise.

"The traders will undsertand from the fact you're insectoids that you'll have excellent credentials for fine detail production. They wouldn't miss the chance!" Z said. "You're gonna get a lot of surprises now!"

"I feel that we have gone many billions of kilometers and have spent nine hundred years in a real and very worthwhile pursuit! We are successful!" Plo cried. "We have found friends, as was our original purpose! We feared that to be true friends we would have to locate other insectoids, but we have found true friends in many forms. Even in machines.

"We will seem emotionless to you, I know. That is not the case. You just do not know how to detect emotion in us."

Lok? Would you please step to the dome to tell me if the separation is going properly? We're almost ready for the seal phase.

They had the ship separated and the Freenz in their quarters exactly on schedule. The regimentation in their society translated into extremely precise planning and execution of any project. Maita sent specialized floaters over to set the moder and to program the flight plan into the ship's computers so no one would need to do anything more. The ship would automatically follow the empire beacons to the one Rollo placed at Freenz. They would arrive in orbit at Freenz in exactly eighty six days, nineteen hours, twelve minutes from engagement of program.

When all the Freenz were aboard and awaiting the moment of launch Maita called all Freenz to attention through the speaker system on the colony ship.

*I have a special message for all the Freenz people. Please give this your closest attention: (Maita translated for Z to announce.)

`Citizens of the United World, I bid you greetings! We have been diligently monitoring the three wavelengths designated nine hundred thirty one years four bliens, two days, and six hours ago in the moral certainty that you have survived and are seeking to return to this, your ancestral home.

`We of the United World feel the greatest pride knowing you have conducted yourselves well in all things and in all meetings with alien lifeforms of many kinds.

''We are proud to claim you, our sisters and brothers! You have served us and your progeny well! You have carried the dream of the Freenz race to a more enlightened and glorious level than we had hoped possible!

`You have returned friends to us here on the United World. You have caused us to join into an alliance with uncountable numbers of differing and strange beings.

''We are all friends and partners, forging into the future with hope – no! More than hope! With the CERTAINTY we are and always will be an important part of the great rhythm of life in the universe! We are no longer alone! We are now and forever a part of a magnificent, bright future for all beings!

`As you return to this, your home world, know you are and will remain the most glorious epic in our history!

'You return our role models and our heroes! Because of you the Freenz race and the United World will also be part of the history of a much greater thing, not merely one world or one star system, but of the entire universe.

`You are the embodiment of our pride! We send to you

our love and our prayers for a safe voyage home.'

This message is directly from Gri Loostris, Queen of the United World.

Z, who was standing in the Freenz ship with Thing sitting astride his shoulder, finally saw a demonstration of emotion by the Freenz. They were nodding vigorously, clacking the top two arms against their "chests" and swaying from side to side. The hard chitin armor made the clacks from a thousand pair of arms deafening. Ziss was next to Z and turned to him after a couple of minutes.

"This is the way we show strong emotion, Z," she said. "It would be much like what Thing described as jumping up and down and cheering among your race. We have fulfilled our duties and will be honored so are naturally very elated. In addition, we have caused our race to fulfill its greatest dream – to become part of a greater thing – to assure the universe we have existed and have done well!

"We extend the thanks of our race to you."

[Zianteus and his friends once stated that the worth of a race could be measured by the extent of its dreams. You have dreamed magnificently. No more need be said. No more can be said.]

"What a beautiful tribute, Thing!" Lok cried.

"Thing has an ability to express what we all feel in a few words," Z said. "I think that expresses it perfectly."

I concur. No more need be said. If Z and Thing will come back here we'll await the Inktan ship with the new drive and complete the course programming and installation of it into the remaining part of the ship. We'll meet again on Freenz to welcome you and your people home. Loostris wants me to convey to you that she feels the officers of this ship should be commended for a very frustrating and difficult job well-done. She's aware far more than most that duty is sometimes terribly frustrating, that one desires nothing more than to be finally free of it. She wants me to convey to you that none knows of your trials more than she, but the moment she was informed you were coming back and were sending many friends in advance made a lifetime of frustration as nothing to the joy of that single moment.

Soon Z and Thing went to Maita to watch as the Freenz ship flashed and was gone.

I really grew to like them. I have to admit that my prejudices would have made me want to smash them on the pretext that they were causing damage to those races they were contacting. I watched your reactions, Z, and learned I can be as much a mountbeast's ass as you can – and I don't even have to try! Thank you for making me mature a little bit. Thing, you were also a deciding factor. Thank you.

[I don't think they'll ever let us down. They understand that they've evolved at less than one quarter of the rate of other types of intelligences, but they are in some important ways much better for it. They caused no real or lasting damage to anyone they met. Louahna's just lazy. She could have spent next to no time and sent us directly to the Freenz, but was so lazy she wanted us to do it all for her so she could lay around Neeahna and get some bedsores on her ass!]

"What?!" Z exclaimed.

"I get this crap from someone who rides around on a floater everywhere it goes?" Louahna said from behind Z. She had stepped through the wall a moment before in plain view of Thing.

[I'm sooooo worried about all those pooooor people on those backward planets! I don't know if pooooooor w'il ol' me can *ever* hope to straighten them out again!] Thing mimicked.

"May your gravity give out when you're ten kilometers over an active volcano," Louahna shot back.

To the elementizer with both of them, Z! Quick!

"All that imitation rubber will gum it up," Z responded.

Louahna stepped into the elementizer, then out again. "That tickles!" she cried.

They played the game for awhile, then Louahna spent some time in private conversation with Maita about the assignment Tab was handling for her. They explored the near area of space while they waited for the Inktan ship to arrive and discovered two more planets. Globe was a nice world with a lot of shallow water and a race of amphibious people who were beginning to build habitats and starting to farm. The second one was a barren rock that Thing christened Barren, [Like Z's love life.]

"Hah! I have a hell of a lot more love life than you do!" Z said.

I don't know, Z. It spends a lot of time down under those oceans wherever we go. I'm not so sure there aren't all kinds of creatures we know nothing about down there! It does spend an inordinate amount of time under the oceans on a lot of worlds!

[On EC, too!]

The Inktan ship arrived. Working with Maita and Z it took five days to install the drive and program it. Maita then sent it on its way and went to New Zule on a direct jump across the two spiral arms between. The Zulians were truly glad to see them and already had a firm trade agreement with the Freenz for precision sensor parts. They wanted very much to meet them.

They then visited Zeena and Tom, an ex-member of the

crew. His mate had just had a second child and they stayed there for ten days, then went back to EC where they caught up on the empire's business while Z made another orchid garden on his island and Thing worked in its undersea gardens.

There were a large number of plants in both of their gardens needing attention. They used the time to get it all in order as best they could.

The camellias were in bloom on the heights, as were the Masdevallias and Odontoglossums in the covering trees. An area of Miltonias was a splash of browns, reds, golds and white and the strange-looking Zygopetalums, Dracula and Maxillarias were beautiful. Thing brought some bright shells from the depths to add to its collection. Some of those shells were among the rarest and most wanted items in the galaxy among collectors, but Thing gave the shells it grew to its friends. They had no need of money! The stones in the bottom of Z's fish pond could buy twenty planets!

The two spent a large percentage of their free time working together. They asked Maita about Tab several times, but Maita said it didn't really know what Tab was doing.

They waited until a few hours before the Freenz were due home, then went to Freenz.

The world was quite dry, but had ample areas of water where beings such as Z and Thing could be comfortable. The Freenz had constructed two large space ports and all the pads were in use. Trade was booming. The Freenz were fast getting a reputation as masters of intricate detail work in any field. They would soon enjoy the elite rating of Zeena, Feach, Qart and New Zule for the finest quality in the galaxy.

The queen, Loostris, got the schematics from Rollo when he was first there for the translating devices and had them installed in all their public buildings. To speak with any citizen of any type one had simply to go to one of the nearby translator machines, punch in the code for the needed languages and speak normally. The devices would translate any number of languages at once, though most traders used Maitan. With the newer machines the Freenz had designed one simply said, "Set" and named the language. If it wasn't a spoken language one could state the code and it would translate. Maita was sure the traders guild would want those machines in all their stations and would eventually have them.

The Freenz were excellent hosts and were honestly deeply interested in others. They were adapted to the dry areas, but were willing to suffer the slight discomforts of humidity and coolness for their guests' comfort. They seemed open and honest.

"I admit to feeling some fears and trepidations when your friend, Rollo, first came here," Queen Loostris explained. "I was by no means certain that our very different types of beings would get along.

"Rollo came from his ship and I was trembling with fear, but when he first took my hand in greeting I knew there was no danger from these people."

Z looked a meaningful look at Thing.

Loostris nodded knowingly. "Yes. He informed me he had hypnotized me when we discussed it later," she continued. "It is a truly fascinating talent! I quail to think what might have happened had I misinterpreted him and caused him harm in my fear! He solved the problem by hypnotizing me and making me like him. My own reaction of trust and friendship relaxed all of my people. We are that way.

"When later Rollo explained what he had done I was glad. It was but a few very short hours after he came here we were being contacted by the traders. It seems to be a rather positive thing we are so slow-developing a race. It prepares us for many useful and needed things. Our acceptance in full membership of an empire we had no thought existed a single day before was amazing to us! We didn't have to pledge any allegiance to anyone or wait for ratification or anything!

"I asked Rollo how we may become members and he asked, `Do you want to join?' and I answered, `Certainly! It is to our sure benefit!'

"He merely said, `Done! You are now a member of the Maitan Empire!' He put a machine here and one at my quarters for us to ask our questions of and said that its placing made us members as soon as we punched the code in to register our world. All I had to do was register the name of the world and receive a fastcom designation code! We don't even have to do what the empire judge machine recommends!

"I will have to pay for the use of the fastcom I understand, as do all users, but the improved translating machines will pay ample royalties to us so we decided there should be a balance and we will, as Rollo suggested, 'call it even.' That will avoid the keeping of millions of useless records.

"It is somewhat strange to our way of thinking that we have virtually no rules to follow as members of the Maitan Empire."

Great exploding galaxies, no! I have enough trouble running an empire without having to enforce a bunch of silly rules! You make your own laws here. If you mess up it's on your own head!

"Are you actually emperor, Maita?" Loostris asked.

[Yeah! He's the emperor! That's why he can't come out here to join us in person. He has far too much work to do and is never allowed to meet anyone. He decided long ago it was best for each person to think that perhaps the emperor is of his own race.]

"Plo and Lok and the rest were on the ship a great part of the time while we were preparing for the trip home," Z added. "They talked with Maita constantly, but never saw him.

"He does that because he says it's better no one knows his race. You're free to suspect he's an insectoid, Rollo's free to think he could be Acnian. Searcher's free to think he's a machine ruler. I can say honestly he's not of my race or Thing's. I won't tell you more."

"Ah! He is not insectoid," Loostris answered. "It would be 'she' if that were the case.

"Searcher is a machine? I must learn of this person! It is a fascinating concept that a machine can be a member of the Maitan Empire! I would greatly enjoy knowing a truly intelligent machine who I could seek answers to questions from! I understand Maita must be at the communications center at all times to run a whole galaxy."

[He doesn't run anything. The machines do. That's why we can go adventuring together. On another level he has to stay in touch because he's responsible and must take command in any emergency. There've been enough of those, I can tell you! It's like Tab says – Tab's a detective and close friend of all of us – about crime. It's rare in the empire, but only one crime of importance every five years on each planet means he would have eight or ten cases a day! Emergencies are usually like that, but the emperor's programmed the machines to handle most of them. There are still things he must handle himself.]

A Feach came into the room to announce it had made contact with the ship. It was exactly on schedule and would arrive in thirty four minutes.

Maita had landed a short distance from the city on the desert. The Freenz told it the returning colony ship was to orbit and what few ships they had would bring the passengers down to the planet. Maita explained the ship was now only a quarter kilometer at its greatest width so could sit right on the surface, then be returned to orbit to be reconnected when the rest of the ship arrived. The Freenz had used a large part of their resources building the ship and had few other smaller ones as a result – even after nine hundred years.

Trade would change that! They would be able to go anywhere in as many ships as they wanted!

Maita had a floater meet the ship as soon as it came into N space, about three light minutes outward from Freenz. The ship would be landed by the floater, as the crew had no training in landing it. It was a good thing this had been arranged because the jubilant Freenz on the ship would have been incapable of handling the job.

The ship landed only a few meters from Maita and, as soon as the outer hatches were opened, the passengers poured out to throw themselves on the ground and roll around, clacking their arms.

"You must forgive their great elation," Queen Loostris said. "It is an emotional time for them."

[I would find it much harder to forgive their NOT feeling elated! I can imagine the emotions I would feel if my ancestors had traveled for so many generations seeking home and found it! I would be insane with joy!]

"Me, too!" Z said. "They spent generations away from home and have returned. I'd do the same!"

After about two hours order was being restored. Ziss and Lok came to the area where Z and Thing waited with Loostris. Lok picked Z up and swung him around.

"Welcome home!" Z greeted.

"Oh, Z! And I once said you would not be able to discern if we were emotional!" she cried. "I did not expect to feel this! It is so strong!"

Thing climbed onto Ziss to enjoy her elation.

[I see you finally arrived home. It's good to see you here where you belong.]

"Oh, Thing! I had never hoped to live to see this beautiful world!" she said. "Oh! It is so beautiful I cannot describe it!"

Well! You two might acknowledge your queen's existence! A little decorum here!

[They're showing as little as possible!]

"They nodded in respect as they approached," Loostris said, suppressing a gurgling sound Maita took for a giggle. "That is all that is required. I am glad they are here and I am proud they are such excellent examples of all that is good in our race. You might easily have met others who were not so good. It gladdens me we had no need of many soldiers. It gladdens me we met with friendship in far places. It gladdens me most my sisters and brothers are home!"

[I sincerely doubt there are many who are not good in your race. It will be all or nothing if you understand Z's sloppy use of the language.]

"She means we might have bred the soldiers at a far greater rate than we did, which well could have changed our patterns of action," Lok explained. "There was that chance at first, but we felt it would be inappropriate to meet others with challenges when we were in need of aid and understanding. We tried to have only enough soldiers to defend should we be attacked.

"Fortunately, we were not."

You seem to have made the wisest choices at each juncture. The only bad thing that happened was in the math. There was too much mass in the ship for the TTH drive to handle. The way you modified it to operate in a partial mode was nothing short of brilliant.

"Then we won't tell you it was done purely by accident," Plo said as she came to join them. "It is good to see you again, Z and Thing.

"Hello, Maita.

"Our ancestors had no other drive and found themselves far from the galaxy and were moving away at an angle from it so an engineer suggested shunting part of the power into the ship's hull to make it an electrical field generator. That would repel the dust that was beginning to collect around the mass of the ship. They did not wish to become an asteroid. That would have encased them and would set their fate to never return to the galaxy of their home.

"When the drive was re-aimed and fired they moved! It was terribly slow when compared to what had taken them outward, but they WERE moving and the ship WAS being steered! They kept it exactly as it was. They were afraid any tinkering would stop the drive altogether. Better slow progress than no progress."

"We are just happy you have returned," Loostris said. "It will take many years to know all that transpired since your leave of Freenz so long ago. Now is the time for us become re-acquainted and to celebrate! No work is to be done on this world for three days. I decree it! All those traders will be forced to wait for trade agreements and to allow us to serve them!

"Three days to honor the heroes of what is beyond doubt the greatest epic of the galaxy!"

That they most surely are. I think the crew should record everything, and it should be filed at Library for all future peoples to read and envy. It was a great thing that was accomplished here.

Everyone began making speeches, but they kept them reasonably short. There were more toasts than speeches. Z and Thing joined with the Feach and Inktans, Momes and Zeenans, Swaz and Bentans and assorted others who were there to celebrate the homecoming of the Great Quest. They stayed until things were relatively back to normal, then returned to EC to wait for the return of either Tab and TR or the remainder of the Freenz ship.

They didn't know what Tab was doing or how long he'd be, but they'd be at one homecoming again, either TR or the Freenz ship. Whichever came first.

Things were finally back to normal – or as normal as ever again they could be.

Being queen of Freenz was not an easy responsibility in the most non-changing of times. Being queen at a time when so many races of so many kinds were coming to Freenz to trade was a virtually impossible task.

It was good her people had not evolved in the same way of those extinct Pweetoos. Their queen must lay all eggs for the brood in addition to doing all the other duties of the station.

The responsibility Loostris felt for each of her people was more than most could bear.

It was well these alien peoples quickly understood what at first many did not: It was by no means a matter of choice that some were farmers, some historians, some scientists and some other things. The eggs were quite different for different ranges of ability. One's choice was whether a given egg would develop into a farmer or main-tenance worker or cleaner, but the choice was not there between queen and scientist or historian and farmer.

Her caring and sense of responsibility was as strong for a cleaner as for a scientist or another queen. More. They were not able to fully take care of themselves.

This fantastic Maitan Empire accepted the Freenz without any least reservations and, instead of condemning them for their differences, studied them, understood them and welcomed them as equals!

Loostris had her fears if others did not. That was part of being queen.

Everyone seemed to treat the inexperienced Freenz

honestly and fairly, even insisting that the machines make the terms of the agreements. She was excessively proud of the abilities of her people to do any kind of labor well. The Zeenans declared the Freenz were as much artists in each detail of what they did as were the Zeenans themselves and even made trade contracts for many parts of their ships.

That was high praise indeed! There was no question Zeena was the most respected world for quality in those products anywhere in the galaxy. Her fears were about all of the contracts coming so suddenly and without depth of experience on her part.

There was also little question the Freenz people were not so adaptable to traumatic change as some. They were doing very well now, but Loostris feared there could be a rapid collapse if some emergency arose they weren't prepared to meet. She would have little choice but to turn to the empire for aid. That would prove devastating to the Freenz, who must have a queen who acted instantly and firmly in every case and who never had a doubt as to the proper course to take in any situation.

She had stated positively and without hesitation or doubt the returning sections of the colony ship would be re-assembled in space and used as a station for research and for delicate parts to be produced in little or no gravity and had suggested use for the mixing and culturing of medicinal products for use at Hospital.

If they only knew!

There were many thousands of worlds in the empire, yet the emperor came in person to rescue a lost colony ship, then delivered a specialized personal communications floater/com to speak directly with her. He would see the ship was placed anywhere she wanted it when the second section arrived.

Lok and the alien, Thing, had spoken about such uses, she had overheard them and stated such would be the role of the ship as though she made up her mind to that many years ago. If it proved any of the ideas were not practical she would have that fact to worry about after giving the impression she had carefully studied the possibilities.

Later, in a private conversation with the emperor through his floater, he said he understood her position and thought she was doing well. No suggestion ever made by Thing was impractical. He often managed to cause Thing to discuss problems where he could listen and could do the same thing. Emperor Maita understood because it was something she had thrust upon her and a thing about which she had no real choice. There were very few who did not think queen or emperor was a glamorous job, but he had been forced to become emperor as much as she was raised to become queen. He knew it was an exhausting, hopeless, frustrating existence and confided he would rather be a dirt farmer or tradesman on an undeveloped world than emperor of the galaxy. Like herself, he wanted nothing more than for the mantle of responsibility to be gone!

He, as she, had no real life of his own. Every minute was for the people.

Certain things simply were not meant to be. Emperor Maita must remain Emperor Maita. Queen Loostris must remain Queen Loostris. That was the way of things.

He understood her and made a pact where he would come to her aid at any time without anyone on Freenz or in the entire Maitan Empire knowing of it. He would in turn feel free to seek her advice on matters she would logically know more about than would he.

She had hopes! If the transition period, which would be quite long in an insect-evolved species, were to pass by successfully, the Freenz would forever be a proud people and would forever be known for the fine quality they produced. It was a part of the race there would never be a lessening of that quality.

Loostris looked slowly around the town from her perch on a roof platform. The sun was warm and the air was dry. There were peoples of four worlds within her view below listening to the tales of the historians.

With a little help and luck this would work!

Maita worked the problem of the Freenz ship again and came to the same conclusion. Get rid of all that mass and it could travel in TTH4.

It called Z to give instructions.

Tab thought of the times he'd answered calls from Wahnee and of the strange adventures he'd had as a result. Now this Louahna was coming up with the same kinds of things.

Tab was turned off at the time except for the plug-in to TR so only free thought was in his mind. TR would join in as it pleased. This was the time they were truly a single entity. They shared a brain.

They had no idea what Louahna wanted this time. It could be anything.

The TR part of the mind agreed with Z that Louahna was lazy and inconsiderate.

Well, it was perfectly true she could locate TR anywhere in the galaxy and take a single step to be aboard with him. She could locate him on the fastcom and save him the trip all the way to Neeahna.

Tab hoped she would give him all the information at hand while TR was cynical enough to assume she would only leave out the more important parts the way she had with the Freenz thing.

Tab would grant she was rather irresponsible while TR said she was playacting and had begun to believe the role was the reality. She was selfish and immature.

Trouble was, she kept forgetting her lines.

It would resolve itself one way or another in time. A straight-out coldblooded planned murder investigation like the one at Castle Drove would be fun now. Maybe something with a real puzzle. Something to make them think.

Neither Tab nor TR wanted anything like the Newlitch Problem though. They'd both had enough of Immins!

TR had a secret love of those times when it could rush in, beams flashing, shields up, damage reports and the terrifying excitement, but more as a fantasy than a reality.

Maybe they were finally through with Immins.

Maybe there were still base planets to be found.

The entire fleet was alerted to trace down any rumors of any kind concerning them and to take no chances. There was no doubt in Maita's mind or anyone else's that if there were any other bases there would be other plots.

It was so tiresome! Every Immin female wanted to be queen of the universe and could lie to herself enough to believe she could become exactly that!

This had nothing to do with Immins. Louahna knew better than to keep such information from Maita. After all, they'd screwed up several of the worlds she was working on.

They would know soon so it wasn't a very productive wonder.

TR said Maita was going to cut the Freenz ship up to install TTH4! They would be home in days!

There was never a dull moment working for (or more

accurately, with) Maita, but both Tab and TR missed being with Z, Thing and the emperor.

Well, hopefully it wouldn't be for long.

Thing listened in fascination as the Freenz historian told of a planet where the people lived in the tops of trees. They farmed and hunted there because the cover was so solid no light reached the ground.

Heku 4 swivelled the ears to listen to the calls of the happy people coming from the forest with the nuts and sweetfruits, then returned to the manuscript written by Heku, father of Heku 1, grandfather of Heku 2, great-grandfather of Heku 3, who was the father of Heku 4. It was Heku, father ancestor four times removed, who taught the people to go to the forest for food in times of drought. Heku 1 had found the Swaz person from another world, a world called Swaville, in the forest.

Friend Brom, the Swaz, and Heku were the legends of the Vood. Friend Brom found the water that never dried up when there were no rains and he found the "eggshells" that were the ship that crashed on Voodworld and from which the Voodians and their food plants and animals were descended.

Friend Brom said certain animals and plants did not fit into what he called "ecological biological chains" on Voodworld.

Friend Brom said it to Heku, so it was true.

Heku had shown Friend Brom the writings of the people of Vood and Friend Brom said it was "digital notation" that was designed for use of "computers".

Friend Brom said it, so it was true.

Heku had written down much of what Friend Brom said

and did and now all other Hekus would continue to study and write about the people of Voodworld until someday another Swaz would come.

Someday, when the people of Voodworld most needed him, the Heku of that time would call and another Swaz would come!

Heku 4 deeply believed that.

Z computed food mass again, added the figures for the water and shook his head.

Enn Far was greatly troubled. Kroon was in another of these endless crises, this time a plague – or a potential one, anyhow.

Sometimes he wondered if it was worth it. He was getting old and tired, had been through one plague, had been leader of the planet, had fought a thousand battles, had been a signatory to the constitution, had worked to establish the court system and the space program and all of it!

Those aliens had come here twenty two years ago (41 Maitan Galactic Standard years) and had started Kroon on the road to salvation – and not in the sense of the ridiculous old-time religions. The Ithian religion had been the major one for all the years since the visit by the Maitans, but there were always new cults cropping up. Call them another kind of plague! At least things didn't seem to go to such extremes anymore, but why couldn't he have one year of true peace in his lifetime!

Was that asking too much? One lousy year?

A little Immin girl on a hidden world on the N arm looked at the sky and dreamed she would someday be queen of the universe!

Her name was Della Foe Capp.

Kene of Teeme, Sorcerer to King Pan of the Kingdom of Lear, studied the Frome, Teel, sitting on the rail-stool across from him.

It was a friend who visited on occasion, staying in Kene's home. The demon, Fael, was another Frome who visited, as was the Targ, Horth.

Wruk, the terrible Pluton demon, closest friend to Kene, told interesting stories of his adventures before Kene and King Lear offered to take any demons back to their homes.

Martin and the wizard, Boss, with his demons, Extrx and Maybe (and the golems) had made such great changes here and had shown the teacher, Tern, that the demons were people from this same world, but the same world was in many places at once and demons could be trapped here.

Boss had taken many demons home. Those demons and their wizard friend had done so much for Tlorg! Almost as much as Martin had done himself!

Boss had also opened Martin's magic box. Only the pure and good could hope to do that.

Kene was the top wizard on Tlorg now and couldn't begin to fathom its secret, though he had opened it for the king – as he must to become what he was.

Now Martin and the others were gone. Martin would return from time to time, but had retired in the Narg Tooth Mountains on the dark continent.

The others may never return. Pity. Kene could use some advice on any number of things – such as how to make a carpet fly!

Bradley Steele, athlete, Terra, looked through the window as the nurse held up his new son. His family had a long tradition as athletes and he was sure little Nigel would continue in that tradition.

Bradley, Nigel and Rodney. That was the traditional naming procedure in the Steele clan. He knew his grandson's name the moment his son was born! He had no doubt the future would know a Nigel Steele, athlete, then a Rod Steele, athlete, just as it now knew a Brad Steele, athlete and would again!

A young magician called Lordrum on a semi-civilized world not far from Earth took an ancient volume from a shelf and reverently opened it.

It held many secrets.

It was always so cold in the castle! Could there be a spell that would make these icy quarters more comfortable for occupation?

Heat: Starting of Fires, Transferring of, Removing – would Transferring bring it here?

He read awhile and shook his head. The old script was much too complicated. It said the effect was temporary, which would do no good.

Bringing! That should be it!

"See Starting of Fires" – damn!

Flashing, Spinning, In Air and Wind, Drawing to Ground.

Maybe removing? Remove it from one place and bring it here!

Removing: "See energy: Grounding of."

That wouldn't be much help to him, but heat was energy in some form or other so maybe an altered spell?

Energy: Bringing of, Transferring of.

That should do it.

Metal wires and mirrors! Damn!

Grounding of will be the same. Alchemy, not magic.

This is an interesting book though. Might as well look it up. Nothing else to do but freeze to death!

Energy: Grounding of. Focus through method two, using clear and unflawed quartz polished into a sphere.... Hey! This is magic!

Use concentration method four, and picture the.... I can do this!

He studied the ancient book for two hours before carefully and thoughtfully putting it back on the shelf. The method wouldn't do him any good with heat, but it might prove useful some day. It was a thing he could keep in his mind.

Keep the book and where to look in mind.

It just might come in handy someday!

The Fethren, Koomthe Klaas, was sweating. He had started this deal on his own and now some big shots from Tltle were going to take it over and there wasn't a thing he could do about it!

It had started as a little recreational drug business he could stay in until he made a bundle and then get out of, but these organized types would see that he didn't get out again! Ever! It was too late!

Where would it all end?

Rimalt was born on Inkta. There were thirty one other Inktans born on Inkta in that same minute so the odds said there would be nothing special about him.

Inkta University Research Department sent an order to Zeena for a research ship the same day and were told T6-RS-ZPC-92728-ME wouldn't be completed for almost ten more years, but the order was placed and noted. Odds were the ship would be a very ordinary – by Zeenan standards –

research ship.

That's the thing about odds.

Professor Klingek of Ternz, working in his laboratory with Linah of Feach, had just completed writing the final results of the tests on the Klariguel spice from Castas four. He had made the test personally five separate times to be absolutely sure the results were no accident.

The research would guarantee safety for billions of beings of reptilian ancestry from all four of the major types of NA8-n plagues known to affect them. It was his hope he could modify the process to make serums for N-type plagues of viral origin that affected any race of any ancestry. There was ample reason to believe he could.

Linah was having the process drilled into her and would be able to carry on the research when he was away for the times he sought other and cheaper basic materials.

Klariguel was prohibitively expensive and wasn't in great supply as some chemicals formed in plants took such exacting conditions they were found in only one place on one world in the entire galaxy.

Kleepepperone was next on the short list and pretest indicated it was going to do the job. It wasn't quite so rare as Klariguel and could be brought in just at the line on price.

It was grown on Kroon and there was a spice company there that could get quantities to handle the demand if there wasn't a serious outbreak, so Klingek agreed to buy it and began to build a reserve of serum.

Meanwhile, he would look at products from other worlds that may be cheaper and more abundant.

Linah gave the report updates to him and said the Kleepepperone was doing the job a little bit better than anticipated so far as she could tell, so there wasn't much point in delaying.

Klingek finished his notations, carefully rechecked them, went completely around the lab to check each and every item in the research, checked Linah's notes against his own, filed the test reports in their proper drawers and went to his office.

He called the budget control officer to tell her he was going to order the plant material (Anything needed in research or in the production of such pharmaceuticals was automatically paid by the empire fund). She gave him a purchase order number, which he placed on fastcom to Kroon along with arrangements for future regular orders until further notice.

He didn't suspect he was also ordering his future murder.

Nekah, a Cheeth girl, was waiting for her future bond-mate, Wilad, to come home. They would finally have the money to go to school and to eventually return home in triumph as bondmates.

They said at home that the vacation worlds would eat them alive and spit them out in little pieces, but this job was for excellent pay and was one where he could earn very large tips. In just two years with her being cashier in the gift shop – that was where she'd heard about the restaurant job and had rushed to com that the job was accepted by her own mate! – she and Wilad would save money for schooling quickly.

They would show those doubters! She had always known she would have high education. Quality, too! Not the regular school she had known back on Chee-il. That prepared her to live as a normal person in a normal society. She was going to prepare herself to live as a special person in high Empire society! She was going to show the doubters on Chee-il that her mate, Wilad, was going to share the best of everything with her!

The future was bright and promising at last. *Nothing* could go wrong now!

Skor He left Venda for Perfect 3. His first trip there. It wouldn't be his last.

Colept checked his supplies, then left Inkta for the outer rim where he was exploring. He was a University trained exobiologist specializing in silicon-based lifeforms which were found only on a few worlds with complex methane/ halogen/ cyanide atmospheres. He would be gone for some time and would be in uncharted areas, but was used to that. He was traveling alone. Not many wanted to face the dangers of what he was doing. The smallest tear in the suit or the least weakness in the plating of the ship and tomorrow would become irrelevant to him.

The ship's sensors were extremely sensitive so he often found anomalous bits and pieces that made no sense. He generally simply cataloged them and forgot them.

He arrived in his search area and began the slow process of locating the planets he sought. Spectrographics, intra/ ultra scans – the whole thing.

There were times when the results weren't conclusive and he twice found new cultures in the stages of develop-ment that would certainly interest the empire. One found communications beams and knew immediately that technology was growing or was soon to be a major factor on that world.

As Colept came into the second system he recorded such a system and located it to find it was from a satellite in orbit above the world.

There was no technology on the ground.

Strange!

It was even stranger when he found the same sort of thing in the next system – and the next!

He moved in closer and stayed to study the satellite in the fourth system and was amazed that the satellite seemed to be of military design and seemed to be aimed toward the planet, not away.

That meant they were designed to keep people ON the worlds, not to protect them!

That was something he would mention to that Swaz detective on Perfect 3 who was known to be working for Emperor Maita directly at times. He could advise the best way to handle the information.

Maybe he would recommend that Colept take it directly to the emperor.

It was certainly strange!

Eenah of Iaft, word seeker, thought about the patterns of the words in the poem she was reading. Somewhat trite was giving it far more credit than it deserved!

Words were great fun. Language was such an imprecise vehicle for communication.

Language: A term used for both vocalized and written communications.

Was: When I mean is.

Such: Unnecessary interjection.

An: = a = one. Silly. Units of speech.

Imprecise: Self-explanatory. It says not precise. The word describes itself in terms of itself so is meaningless.

Vehicle: Like that blimp? Talk about imprecise!

For: As opposed to against, I presume.

Communication: That which the sentence failed to accomplish!

All that without breaking down the words of the first word's explanation. A good seeker can take almost anything one says and quickly define it as being anything she chooses. That is hardly diplomatic. Eenah wondered if there was even a slight possibility her odd talent would come to any use whatever.

The universe in which all of this took place doesn't observe or note such things. It doesn't care.

C. D. Moulton's works are available on most major outlets as printed or e-books. CD writes the CD Grimes, PI, mysteries, the Det. Lt. Nick Storie mysteries, the Clint Faraday mysteries, the Flight of the Maita science fiction series, books on orchid culture and many others of many types. Mystery, adventure, intrigue, science fiction, humor, fantasy, paranormal, mild erotica, and factual.